NEW YORK REVIEW
CLASSICS

M000209495

# NADA

JEAN-PATRICK MANCHETTE (1942–1995) was a genre-redefining French crime novelist, screenwriter, critic, and translator. Born in Marseilles to a family of relatively modest means, Manchette grew up in a southwestern suburb of Paris, where he wrote from an early age. While a student of English literature at the Sorbonne, he contributed articles to the newspaper *La Voie communiste* and became active in the national students' union. In 1961 he married, and with his wife, Mélissa, began translating American crime fiction—he would go on to translate the works of such writers as Donald Westlake, Ross Thomas, and Margaret Millar, often for Gallimard's Série Noire. Throughout the 1960s Manchette supported himself with various jobs writing television scripts, screenplays, young-adult books, and film novelizations. In 1971 he published his first novel, a collaboration with Jean-Pierre Bastid, and embarked on his literary career in earnest, producing ten subsequent works over the course of the next two decades and establishing a new genre of French novel, the *néo-polar* (distinguished from the traditional detective novel, or *polar*, by its political engagement and social radicalism). During the 1980s, Manchette published a celebrated translation of Alan Moore's *Watchmen* graphic novel for a *bande-dessinée* publishing house co-founded by his son, Doug Headline. In addition to *Fatale*, *The Mad and the Bad*, and *Ivory Pearl* (all available from NYRB Classics), Manchette's novels *Three to Kill* and *The Prone Gunman*, as well as Jacques Tardi's graphic-novel adaptations of them (titled *West Coast Blues* and *Like a Sniper Lining Up His Shot*, respectively), are available in English.

DONALD NICHOLSON-SMITH's translations of noir fiction include Manchette's *Three to Kill*, Thierry Jonquet's *Mygale* (a.k.a. *Tarantula*), and (with Alyson Waters) Yasmina Khadra's *Cousin K*. He has also translated works by Paco Ignacio Taibo II, Henri Lefebvre, Raoul Vaneigem, Antonin Artaud, Jean Laplanche, Guillaume Apollinaire, and Guy Debord. For NYRB he has translated Manchette's *Fatale*, *Ivory Pearl*, and *The Mad and the Bad* (winner of the French-American Foundation Translation Prize for Fiction in 2014), and Jean-Paul Clébert's *Paris Vagabond*, as well as the French comics *The Green Hand* by Nicole Claveloux and *Yellow Negroes and Other Imaginary Creatures* by Yvan Alagbé. Born in Manchester, England, he is a longtime resident of New York City.

LUC SANTE is the author of *Low Life*, *Evidence*, *The Factory of Facts*, *Kill All Your Darlings*, *Folk Photography*, and, most recently, *The Other Paris*. He translated Félix Fénéon's *Novels in Three Lines* and has written introductions to several other NYRB Classics, including *Vagabond Paris* by Jean-Paul Clébert and *Pedigree* by Georges Simenon. A frequent contributor to *The New York Review of Books*, he teaches writing and the history of photography at Bard College.

# NADA

JEAN-PATRICK MANCHETTE

*Translated from the French by*
DONALD NICHOLSON-SMITH

*Introduction by*
LUC SANTE

NEW YORK REVIEW BOOKS

*New York*

THIS IS A NEW YORK REVIEW BOOK
PUBLISHED BY THE NEW YORK REVIEW OF BOOKS
435 Hudson Street, New York, NY 10014
www.nyrb.com

Library of Congress Cataloging-in-Publication Data
Names: Manchette, Jean-Patrick, 1942–1995, author. | Nicholson-Smith,
  Donald, translator.
Title: Nada / by Jean-Patrick Manchette ; translated by Donald Nicholson-
  Smith.
Other titles: Nada. English
Description: New York : New York Review Books, [2019] | Series: New York
  Review Books classics.
Identifiers: LCCN 2018046763 (print) | LCCN 2018051233 (ebook) |
  ISBN 9781681373188 (epub) | ISBN 9781681373171 (pbk. : alk. paper)
Classification: LCC PQ2673.A452 (ebook) | LCC PQ2673.A452 N313 2019
  (print) | DDC 843/.914—dc23
LC record available at https://lccn.loc.gov/2018046763

ISBN 978-1-68137-317-1
Available as an electronic book; ISBN 978-1-68137-318-8

Printed in the United States of America on acid-free paper.
10  9  8  7  6  5  4  3  2

# INTRODUCTION

*NADA*, FIRST published in November 1972, was the fourth novel by Jean-Patrick Manchette, not counting pseudonymous titles, novelizations of films, and other products of what he called "industrial" writing. He was twenty-nine and a seasoned Grub Street professional, and he was fully aware of the political currents of his time. He had joined Communist youth organizations a decade earlier and demonstrated in favor of the liberation of Algeria; more recently he had come under the influence of the Situationist International. It was natural, especially in the highly politicized cultural climate of post-'68 France, that he should merge his two reigning passions and begin writing thrillers on political themes. The first novel he wrote under his own name, *L'Affaire N'Gustro* (1971), was based on the kidnapping and disappearance of the Moroccan opposition leader Mehdi Ben Barka in Paris in 1965.

*Nada* is also about a kidnapping—of the U.S. ambassador to France by a ragtag bunch known as the Nada group, led by professional revolutionaries. The book is structured like a classic caper novel by Frédéric Dard or Albert Simonin. American readers, encountering it in Donald Nicholson-Smith's crisp and astute translation, might consider it a cousin to the novels that Donald Westlake (whom Manchette admired and translated) wrote under the pseudonym

Richard Stark, most of which involve capers gone wrong; like them it is dry and tight, and the pages fly by as if the reader were watching a movie. The caper format is here adapted to the single most newsworthy leftist-terrorist scenario of the 1970s: the symbolic abduction. The casual reader, unburdened by dates, might think that *Nada* was inspired by the kidnapping of Hanns Martin Schleyer by the Red Army Faction in Germany, or that of Aldo Moro by the Red Brigades in Italy, but those events would not occur until 1977 and 1978, respectively.

*Nada* was written early in the period that became known in Europe as the Years of Lead, a time when revolutionary fervor was cresting, as was frustration at the glacial if not retrograde pace of social change. The urge to action was felt everywhere, although it primarily resulted in meetings and pamphlets. But the Red Brigades carried out their first kidnapping in 1972—the twenty-minute abduction of a factory foreman—and the Red Army Faction also undertook a bombing campaign that year: four incidents, five dead, fifty-four injured. (The French counterparts of these groups, notably Action Directe, would not be formed for several more years.) Manchette recorded in his diary that on May 7, as he was finishing the manuscript, his wife (and frequent collaborator), Mélissa Manchette, suggested that his characters might be "positive models," to which he responded: "Politically, they are a public hazard, a true catastrophe for the revolutionary movement. The collapse of leftism into terrorism is the collapse of the revolution into spectacle."

The characters in the gang are the usual odd mix you expect to find in caper novels. Buenaventura Diaz is one sort of professional revolutionary, an exile who never met his

father—he died in 1937 defending the Barcelona Commune—
and who has invested his whole life in militant action; his
only other significant interest is gambling at cards. In Claude
Chabrol's uneven 1974 film adaptation he is given the full
spaghetti-western romantic treatment. André Épaulard is a
professional of another sort, a former member of the Communist Resistance during the Occupation who has never
been able to quench his thirst for action, and while pursuing
revolutionary opportunities around the world has also dabbled in corruption. Manchette enjoys endowing his characters with Homeric epithets; Épaulard is usually "the
fifty-year-old" or "the ex-FTP fighter," referring to the "Francs-
Tireurs et Partisans" in the Resistance. His name implies
that he is given to shouldering his way through. In his review
of Chabrol's film, Andrew Sarris noted that the character's
essence combines Humphrey Bogart's "wrinkled fatalism"
and Yves Montand's "wistful patience."

Marcel Treuffais, who teaches philosophy at a suburban
lycée, is the author of the Nada manifesto, their resident
intellectual, a proud member of the Libertarian Association
of the Fifteenth Arrondissement (Errico Malatesta Group).
In keeping with genre conventions, there is also muscle: the
driver, D'Arcy, a drunk (he is invariably referred to as "the
alcoholic"); and Meyer, a waiter who has a crazy wife, seems
to have gotten involved with the group for no particular
reason, and doesn't do much ("Meyer, who hardly ever said
anything"). There is also an unofficial sixth member, Véronique Cash, the group member who provides the farm they
use as a hideout, who proves to be as ferocious a fighter as
Diaz and much more so than Épaulard. As she tells the latter: "My cool and chic exterior hides the wild flames of a

burning hatred for a techno-bureaucratic capitalism whose cunt looks like a funeral urn and whose mug looks like a prick."

Manchette is as ever rich in details; as always, he flaunts his encyclopedic knowledge of guns and cars. And he is sharp in his satire of both the faction-intensive Parisian left of the time and the labyrinthine corridors of the government and the police. Few thrillers have been stuffed with quite as many acronyms as this one. It is telling that a major plot turn occurs as a result of an obscure squabble between two law-enforcement agencies. For that matter, every action and statement by the gang is followed by retorts and denunciations by the variegated leftist groupuscules, which are duly noted by *Le Monde* in a sidebar. An entity calling itself the New Red Army dismisses them as "petty-bourgeois nihilists" and proclaims:

> "Down with All Little Neumanns!"
>
> "Neumann? You mean like Alfred E. Neuman?" asked Épaulard in alarm.
>
> "Heinz Neumann," Cash clarified, placing the tray and radio on the table. "A guy who had something to do with the Canton Commune in December 1927."

From its tower *Le Monde* parses their manifesto: "The style is disgusting...and the childishness of certain statements of an archaic and unalloyed anarchism might raise a smile in other circumstances." TREMBLE RICH PEOPLE YOUR PARIS IS SURROUNDED WE ARE GOING TO BURN IT DOWN says a wall, echoing the telegrams sent from the occupied Sorbonne to the Communist Parties of China and the USSR during May '68: SHAKE IN YOUR

SHOES BUREAUCRATS STOP THE INTERNATIONAL POWER OF THE WORKERS COUNCILS WILL SOON WIPE YOU OUT STOP.... Meanwhile a member of the ambassador's protective detail is reading *Ramparts* and the other *The Greening of America* by Charles Reich.

The book is briskly paced, full of clipped dialogue and nonstop action, but it also presents a political argument. Treuffais, who seems to be something of an authorial proxy, decides not to go along with the plot, for doctrinal reasons: "Terrorism is only justified when revolutionaries have no other means of expressing themselves and when the masses support them." By the end, Diaz, who had kicked Treuffais out of his apartment when the teacher begged off, has come to agree with him. "Leftist terrorism and State terrorism, even if their motivations cannot be compared, are the two jaws of . . . the same mug's game," he admits. "The desperado is a commodity." Manchette has the press dub the gang's hideout "the tragic farmhouse"—the epithet used by the newspapers in 1912 to refer to the death scene of Jules Bonnot, the driver and press-appointed leader of the Bonnot Gang, an earlier model of that commodity. Sixteen years after its French publication, in his preface to the book's first Spanish edition, Manchette acknowledged that its political argument was "insufficient and obsolete," because it "isolated" the gang from the broader oppositional social movement, and furthermore failed to account for the "direct manipulation" to which the State would have subjected such a group.

But whatever its theoretical shortcomings, *Nada* is a remarkable book. At the time of its publication, there was nothing like it outside of Manchette's work; novels and politics kept separate bedrooms. As Didier Daeninckx, who began writing his political thrillers in the 1980s, put it in an interview: "Manchette seized a scorned genre that in the 1960s was right-wing, even extreme right-wing, and in one stroke shattered the conventions. With that he effected a split in the genre." Manchette essentially launched an industry of left-wing thrillers, ranging from a historically minded stylist such as Daeninckx to the brew of crime, porn, and agitprop served up by Éditions de la Brigandine in their quickies, which are bylined with various noms de guerre and intended to lure the innocent consumer of pulp. Manchette himself would go on to produce six more novels in the course of the 1970s, each seemingly more complex and considered than the one before. But *Nada* was his first real hit, as in a hit song, striking an unexpected chord that resonated with the French reading public, and like a true hit it has carried on, bringing the baggage of its time into our own very different set of circumstances without losing any of its power.

—Luc Sante

## Translator's Acknowledgments

I MUST once again thank Doug Headline for answering my questions, not to mention his ongoing (and patient) support for our translation of his father's cycle of noir novels from the 1970s. Once again too, let me say how grateful I am to Alyson Waters, my partner in this endeavor, to all at New York Review Books, and to Gregory Nipper for his copyediting. Jim Brook cast a critical eye on the translation and made many suggestions—thank you, Jim. As usual, words cannot adequately express my debt to Mia Nadezhda Rublowska, without whom—well, without whom.

—D. N.-S.

# NADA

The heart that beats for the welfare of mankind passes therefore into the rage of frantic self-conceit, into the fury of consciousness to preserve itself from destruction; and to do so by casting out of its life the perversion that it really is.

—HEGEL

That is how things are, and inasmuch as one sometimes has to shoot, one may as well do so cleanly, without the drawbacks of a high caliber and a wide-spreading pattern. Cleanly? Well, an impeccable kill must be the chief concern of the good hunter. That is our essential point. In the chapter on shooting we shall see what imperatives, in our view, arise from this principle. For the moment, suffice it to say that a bore is preferable which is just slightly more than adequate.

—LE CHASSEUR FRANÇAIS

# I

Dearest Mom,

This week I am not waiting till Saturday to write to you because do I have things to tell you, my gosh yes!!! The fact is, those Anarchists who kidnapped the U.S. Ambassador, well, it was us who got them, our squad I mean. I must say right away that I myself did not kill a single one. I want to be clear on that because I know it would ~~disterb dissturb~~ be very upsetting for you, my darling Mom. All the same, let me say again that this is something that has to be faced head on, just in case one day we have to use force in defense of the State. Turning the other cheek is all very well, but what do you do, I ask you, when you are dealing with people who want to destroy everything? Father Castagnac pretty much agrees with me (in fact we studied the question the other Sunday when I went over after mass). His opinion is that if policemen are not ready for anything, like I am, there would be no reason for certain individuals not to do anything they want and that is my own point of view too. Seriously, my sweet Mom, would you want a country with no police? Would you want the Barquignats' boy (just taking him as an example) to lay his foul hands on your daughter, who is also my sister? Would you want our property, which we worked so hard for, overrun by levelers and collectivists in an orgy of destruction? I am not saying that the majority of people in our town are not decent folk, but still, even in this peaceful rural community, if it were not known that there is a police force, and one ready to shoot if need be, I can think of a few who would not hesitate, not to mention the Gypsies.

Anyway, yesterday, all I did was do my job. I was with François, who I have told you about, and we fired quite a lot, but to no effect. It was other police officers on the other side of the building who eventually got inside the place and managed to kill the individuals. I will not dwell on a bloody slaughter fit to turn your stomach. François is sorry he did not get hold of one of the anarchists himself and give them a taste of what they deserved. Personally I would not go that far, but I respect his point of view.

This has been a long letter and I do not quite know what else to tell you. So I will close for today. Kiss my father for me, Nadège too. I hold you tight, next to my heart.

Your loving son,
Georges Poustacrouille

P.S. Could you, if it is not too much trouble, send me the camembert-box drum because I will need it as we are having a surprise party for Sergeant Sanchez's promotion. Thank you in advance.

# 2

ÉPAULARD parked his Cadillac half on the sidewalk and then walked up the street as far as the urinal on the corner by the mosque and the Jardin des Plantes and relieved himself. Retracing his steps, he lit a filtered Française as he walked. He was a tall thin man with the mug of an army doctor, an iron-gray crew cut, and a beige raincoat with epaulets. He went into a wine store that was also a bar and ordered a Sancerre, which he savored. Or at least as best he could, considering that smoking sixty cigarettes a day does not leave you much of a palate.

It was five past noon. D'Arcy was late. At that moment the young man came in. He struck the shoulder of the beige raincoat with the palm of his hand.

"Ciao."

"Hi."

"I have an appointment at two and I haven't eaten. Is your car far away?"

"Just over the way," said Épaulard as he settled up.

They crossed the street. There was already a ticket under the Cadillac's windshield wiper. Épaulard tossed it into the gutter. They got into the mud-spattered white car.

"Have you been back in France long?" asked D'Arcy.

"Three weeks."

"Have you seen the guys?"

"Nobody."

"What are you up to just now?"

As he was speaking, D'Arcy had opened the glove compartment and was rooting in it.

"It's in the door cubby," said Épaulard.

D'Arcy reached down and brought out a slim silver flask and drank directly from it. He had a red face. He was sweating. Same old boozer, thought Épaulard. When D'Arcy had finished drinking, the fifty-year-old put the flask away. Engraved on it was a bird devouring a snake and a legend in ornate lettering: *Salud y pesetas y tiempo para gustarlos.*

"You've been in Mexico," observed D'Arcy.

"I've been pretty much all over. Algeria, Guinea, Mexico."

"And Cuba."

"Yes, Cuba."

"They kicked you out," said D'Arcy.

Épaulard nodded.

"And what are you doing now?" D'Arcy asked again.

"You're beginning to piss me off," said Épaulard. "Just what is it you want?"

"Some comrades and I," said D'Arcy, "are in need of an expert."

"Expert in what? I'm an expert in lots of things."

"These comrades and me," said D'Arcy, "we are going to snatch the U.S. Ambassador to France."

Épaulard got out of the car and slammed the door violently. He went back across the street. D'Arcy ran after him. A nasty cold drizzle was beginning.

"Don't be a fool," said the alcoholic. "I haven't finished explaining."

"I don't want to hear any more. Fuck off!"

Épaulard went back into the wine shop and ordered another Sancerre. D'Arcy hovered unhappily in the doorway.

"Okay then, go screw yourself," he said at last, and went off.

# 3

"WHICH is why," concluded Treuffais, "we can say with Schopenhauer that 'the solipsist is a madman imprisoned in an impregnable citadel.' Does anyone have a question?"

Nobody did. The bell rang. With a gesture, Treuffais sought vainly to quiet the hubbub that immediately engulfed the classroom.

"Next time," he said, raising his voice, "we'll examine contemporary rationalism and its variants. I need a volunteer for a presentation on Gabriel Marcel."

Two hands went up.

"I wish it wasn't always the same ones," said Treuffais sarcastically. "Mister Ducatel, tell me, are you perhaps very busy this weekend?"

"Yeah," replied the student in a mischievous way. "I'm going hunting."

"Hunting to hounds, I imagine," ironized Treuffais.

"Yes, sir."

"All the same, you'll prepare the presentation on Gabriel Marcel. For Monday. Everyone may leave the room very quietly."

The horde of brats left the room very noisily. Treuffais snapped his briefcase shut, listening to the fading footfalls of their expensive clodhoppers. He left Saint-Ange Academy by a side door. At that moment Ducatel's Ford Mustang passed, revving and spraying Treuffais's pants with muddy water. Ducatel screeched to a halt and got halfway out of his car.

"I'm so sorry, sir," he offered. But he could not conceal his mirth.

"You stupid shit!" said Treuffais.

"Watch your language," replied Ducatel venomously.

But Treuffais had turned his back on him and was getting into his Citroën 2CV across the street. The young philosophy teacher drove quickly out of Bagneux, reached Porte d'Orléans and took the outer boulevards westward. He reckoned he was at risk of losing his job. Ducatel would complain to his daddy that he had been insulted. The daddy in question would then pass this on to the director, Monsieur Lamour, who incidentally had a face like a road accident.

"You might as well be called Mister Bouillon" said Treuffais to his gearshift. "And give your name to your institution: Mister Bouillon of Cours Bouillon."

The traffic light turned green.

"Screw it all!" added Treuffais.

A car horn beeped behind him. Treuffais leant out of his open window.

"French Schweinehunde," he shouted. "We focked you in 1940 and we will fock you again!"

An office worker in a leather jacket on a moped sprang from his bike and dashed toward the 2CV. Nervously, Treuffais apprehensively pulled his window shut. The moped rider pounded on the door's metal paneling with his fist. He resembled Raymond Bussières.

"Get out, asshole!" he shouted.

Treuffais unlocked a switchblade and opened the car door. He pointed the knife at the aggressor.

"Gonna kill you, man!" he said in would-be Hollywood black English. "Use your guts for suspenders!"

The office worker got the general drift, leapt backwards, stumbled over his Solex and fell flat on his face. Treuffais started up, laughing, went through the light on orange and sped on his own down Boulevard Lefebvre.

"*Sono* schizo," he said. "And polyglot! *Primoque in limine Pyrrhus exultat.*"

He found a parking spot on Rue Olivier-de-Serres, a few steps from his place. In the elevator he heard the phone ringing inside the apartment. He hurried to get in and answer it. It was D'Arcy on the line.

"What about your expert?" asked Treuffais.

"He won't do it," said D'Arcy.

"We'll do without him."

"That's too bad."

"We'll manage. Excuse me, the doorbell is ringing."

"Okay, I'm hanging up. I'll call you back."

"Don't bother. We'll see each other tonight."

"Right. Till tonight then."

"Tonight."

Treuffais hung up and went to the door.

A short guy, but broad, with wavy hair, about twenty-five, which was Treuffais's own age, was holding out a vile glossy brochure.

"We are coming around as we do every year," the man said. "From the Federation of Breton Scholarship Medical Students."

"Go fuck yourself," suggested Treuffais, pushing him away with the palm of his hand.

"Hey, hold on, buddy!"

"I'm not your buddy!" cried Treuffais with ferocity and

angrily shoved the Breton scholarship recipient again. The man batted at him with his literature. Treuffais delivered a left to the kidney. The hawker dropped his publications. A kick from Treuffais scattered them on the stairs.

"You bastard!" shouted the student. "I have to make a living."

"A big mistake!" exclaimed Treuffais as he used both hands to push the Breton backwards down the stairwell, where he ended up on his back howling in clearly genuine and acute pain.

Treuffais went back into his apartment and slammed the door. The telephone rang again. The young man hurriedly opened a bottle of Kronenbourg and lit a cigarette before picking up.

"Marcel Treuffais speaking."

"Buenaventura Diaz."

"Awake already?"

"That idiot D'Arcy called me. So, just like that, his crappy expert backed out."

"Yeah, just like that. But it doesn't matter."

"I don't agree," replied Buenaventura Diaz. "The guy is in the picture now. We have to see what he has for balls."

"Oh, just drop it."

"I'll go and see him tonight. You with me?"

"What are you going to tell him?

"To keep his trap shut."

"Let it go," counseled Treuffais again.

"No."

"Suit yourself. What about the meeting?"

"I might be late."

"All right."

"Anything else?" asked the Catalan.

"Nothing. You?"

"Nothing."

"Okay. Bye then."

"Bye."

Treuffais hung up and started opening his mail. Marie-Paule Schmoulu and Nicaise Hourgnon are delighted to inform you that...Well, holy shit, the poor kid has finally got shacked up. Next envelope. Prices slashed at Radieuse and Co.! Treuffais opened the brochure and contemplated "stylish country-style bookshelves" before tossing the advertising into the wastebasket and going to open a second beer. He was shaking with rage. He went and sat down in the large armchair. Horsehair poked through holes in the leather worn out by his father's backside. The carpet in front of the chair was threadbare, worn out by his father's feet. Treuffais unsealed another envelope bearing a thirty-centime stamp. Annual dinner of the Fifteenth Arrondissement Libertarian Association (Errico Malatesta Group). A discussion led by Comrade Parvulus would follow the meal: "Libertarians and the Jewish-Arab Conflict: A Few Remarks Based on Plain Common Sense." Bullshit. Treuffais screwed the announcement up into a ball and flung it to the far end of the room. The last item was a postcard. Recto: Rice Cultivation near Abidjan. Verso: "May 12. Dear Old Pal: Still won't be home this year. Probably won't be home ever. You should join me. I've caught the clap from the daughter of a chief. I'd be happy to pass it on to you whenever you like. Fuck you royally. Popaul."* Treuffais stuck the card in a drawer of the family sideboard, finished his beer and went for lunch at the local café.

---

*Popaul, a nickname for Paul, is also a nickname for a penis.

# 4

AFTER lunch, Meyer had an argument with his wife, which ended as usual: Annie tried to strangle him.

"Stop, for God's sake!" cried Meyer, but she was crushing his pharynx. So he pawed around on the table, which was within his reach, and managed to grab a glass bottle of Évian, three-quarters full. He landed a light blow with it on the young woman's head by way of a warning shot. Annie was in full crisis mode. She did not relax her grip. She sank her nails into Meyer's neck. He sighed in desperation, then let fly. At the third blow Annie let go, clapped her hands to her head and rolled onto the floor screaming.

"Come on, sweetheart," said Meyer. "Come on."

Annie was wailing. He covered his ears.

"Shit!" he roared.

He rushed into the bathroom and threw water on his face. Raising his head, he saw in the little mirror that Annie had left deep scratches on both sides of his neck. They were bleeding. He splashed alcohol on the wounds, and his eyes teared up. The blood continued to ooze. Quick. Meyer took his white shirt off, but too late: the collar was stained. He looked at himself in the glass once more. He saw a twenty-three-year-old guy, blond and doughy, with little eyes the color of shucked oysters. He had gooseflesh. He powdered his neck to absorb the blood. In the next room, he could hear Annie banging her head against the wall. He went to join her.

"Come on, baby, stop it. I love you."

"Just die, slimeball," Annie replied. "You dirty Jew," she added, "I hate you. I'm going to go to Belleville and get myself fucked by Africans. I'm going to get screwed," she insisted quite violently.

She rubbed her head and started weeping with pain. Her hair was beautiful and fine. Meyer wanted to shoot himself or just go to work—it was hard to say which. He looked at his watch. Two fifteen. Just time enough to avoid being late.

Annie suddenly stopped crying and got to her feet.

"I made a nice drawing last night."

"Would you show it to me?"

"No. I hate you. You're a piece of shit."

"Please, sweetheart," said Meyer.

"All right, all right," said Annie in an uncouth way. "I'll go and get it for you."

While she was in the other room, Meyer wiped his neck a final time and put on a clean shirt and a black clip-on bow tie. He slipped into a threadbare velvet jacket. He would not don his waiter's white jacket until he got to the brasserie.

Annie came back with a large watercolor depicting a fort in the desert. Little men wearing outsize pith helmets seemed to be trying to mount an attack on the fortress, but without success: Annie had painted a mass of brown blobs raining down on them.

"Those are turds of Africans," the young woman explained. "That is my house."

"Very pretty," said Meyer.

Annie looked at the alarm clock.

"Darling," she exclaimed, "you have to leave right away. You're going to be late."

"Yes," said Meyer, "I'm off."

"I'm sorry about before. I'll be better tonight. I'll take some Gardenal."

"Don't take too much," counseled Meyer.

At the door he turned around.

"I'll be late this evening. I have my meeting."

"You'll tell me about it."

"I will," he lied.

"I'm sorry I lost my temper. Don't know what came over me. It's nerves."

"It doesn't matter at all. Forgive me for hitting you with the bottle."

"I love you."

"Same here," said Meyer and left.

He arrived at his job five minutes late. The brasserie, near Montparnasse Station, was bustling. Meyer put on his waiter's coat and got straight to work.

"Coming through!"

"Cut yourself shaving again?" the cashier, Mademoiselle Labeuve, asked him ironically.

"No," replied Meyer. "This time it's eczema. When I get eczema, I can't help it, I have to scratch."

Mademoiselle Labeuve contemplated Meyer with disgust. He kept on working. He thought about the night's meeting, and this helped him relax somewhat.

# 5

AFTER his telephone call to Treuffais, Buenaventura had gone back to sleep for a while. He was dragged from his slumber at three in the afternoon by his alarm clock. He sat up in bed in his underwear, his mouth furry. He had smoked, drunk and played poker until five in the morning. He rubbed his eyes with his fists. He stripped, went into the bathroom, washed his feet, underarms and crotch, brushed his teeth, and shaved. Then he slipped on corduroy pants and a turtleneck sweater darned at the elbows. Back in the bedroom he tidied up a little, made the bed, took dirty glasses to the sink, and stood empty liter wine bottles against the wall near the door. A plastic cup held a remnant of Margnat. Buenaventura tossed the wine down, shuddered horribly and almost threw up. He opened his shutters and looked out over Rue de Buci. Long-haired students were chatting on canopied café terraces. Buenaventura closed the windows once more, then gathered up wine-stained playing cards scattered on a little folding table and tossed them into a wastebasket. Must remember to buy a dozen certified decks. He sat down on his bed and did his accounts in a notebook. That night he had won 573 francs. Good. A streak of bad luck seemed to be ending. Buenaventura needed an overcoat or at least a peacoat. The weather was turning cold.

He put the money away, dividing it among the various

mended pockets of his pants and those of his leather coat, which was musty and full of holes. He put on unwashed socks and rubber boots, got into his coat, wound a black scarf around his neck and covered his head with a black felt hat made before the Second World War in Harrisburg, Pennsylvania. With his thin pale face and bushy muttonchops he looked like a brigand in a neorealist version of *Carmen*.

Leaving the Longuevache Hotel, he walked to D'Arcy's place, a tiny studio kitchenette in a building with an unrestored façade in Rue Rollin near Place de la Contrescarpe. He knocked.

"Yeah?" shouted the alcoholic. "It's not locked!"

"It's me," Buenaventura announced prudently, pushing the door open.

On one of his good days, D'Arcy might have been crouched behind the door, hammer in hand and ready to strike. Buenaventura entered, relieved to see the drunkard at the back of the room, stretched out on his couch with a bottle of Mogana on his belly.

The floor was barely visible beneath a thick layer of crushed food scraps and cigarette butts. In the kitchen area Buenaventura spotted coffee simmering in a saucepan. He poured himself a glass, swatted an ant on the rim of a sugar bowl, and made for the telephone.

"I was dreaming I was getting a blow job," said D'Arcy distractedly.

Buenaventura did not respond. He thumbed through an address book by the phone and found someone named Épaulard. D'Arcy was staring at the ceiling.

"I must write to my mother," he said, "and ask her to send money. You couldn't lend me a few shekels, could you?"

Buenaventura chuckled and emptied his glass.

"Thanks for the coffee. See you tonight."

"You're taking off?" asked D'Arcy in surprise.

But the Catalan was already gone, setting off on foot in a northeasterly direction.

On Boulevard Saint-Michel he was stopped by a man in a blue coat.

"Police. Your papers."

The man was showing his cop ID. Buenaventura would gladly have punched him in the face, but a group of sixty armed and helmeted CRS riot police was stationed not far away near the fountain.* The Catalan produced his alien resident card.

"Profession?"

"Musician."

"It says 'student' here," said the cop, pointing with a fat finger at the relevant entry.

"The card is from a while ago. I was a student at that time."

"Better get it updated."

"Yes, sir."

The cop returned the card to Buenaventura.

"All right then."

The Catalan went on his way, still on foot; the days were long gone when you could ride for free on the bus by washing off the stamp on used tickets. Walking briskly, Buenaventura soon reached Rue Rouget-de-Lisle near the Tuileries. He entered the building where Épaulard lived and consulted the list of tenants posted on the window of the concierge's door. He climbed two flights of stairs. A door bore a new

---

*Compagnies Républicaines de Sécurité: mobile reserve police force, part of France's National Police under the aegis of the minister of the interior.

copper plaque that read ANDRÉ ÉPAULARD—LEGAL COUNSEL. The door had a peephole. Buenaventura blocked it with a finger and rang the bell. He heard movement inside.

"What is it?" came a male voice.

"Guess!" said Buenaventura merrily.

The lock turned. The door opened halfway. Buenaventura gave it a good kick. It flew open and struck the fifty-year-old in the chest, and he fell backwards. Buenaventura entered brusquely, slamming the door behind him. His victim reacted far more quickly than he had expected, grabbing his ankle and causing him to fall. Taken by surprise, Buenaventura let fly with a kick that missed its target. His ears were seized and his head slammed against the wall.

"Have you quite finished, you little shit?"

Buenaventura looked at the fifty-year-old man. Both adversaries were visibly astonished.

"Thomas!" exclaimed the Catalan.

"Carlos!"

"I'm not called Carlos now," said Buenaventura as he got to his feet.

"And I'm not Thomas," said Épaulard. "I am André Épaulard. In fact that's my real name."

"Buenaventura Diaz," said the Catalan. "And that's my real name too."

"You can't make this stuff up," observed Épaulard. "What got into you, laying into me like that?"

"I had no idea it was you."

"I don't get it. Come have a drink. And explain."

The two men walked down the hallway and into a study with a heavy desk and two leather armchairs. Against the wall stood a khaki metal cabinet. Épaulard opened it and took out a bottle of Polish vodka and two glasses. He sat down at the desk and Buenaventura took one of the armchairs.

"Been a while," said Buenaventura.

"Since '62."

"What the hell have you been up to?"

"Algiers. Working on the program with the Pabloists."*

"Idiot."

"You still an anarchist?"

"As you can tell."

"Jesus Christ!" exclaimed Épaulard suddenly. "Don't tell me you're involved with a certain D'Arcy?"

"Yes, I am."

"On that ambassador operation?"

"That's right."

"You're fucked," said Épaulard. "As for D'Arcy, he's a complete alkie. You shouldn't go near him."

"That's debatable."

"Not with me. But tell me why you are here and why you laid into me. My tender soul wants to know."

"It's simple. D'Arcy was supposed to find us a specialist. A certain André Épaulard. I had no idea it was you. When D'Arcy said his specialist was backing out, I came over here to pay him a visit—just to make doubly sure that he wouldn't blab about our plans."

"That's ridiculous. Once news is out, it's out."

"Well, anyway, no harm done."

"You really mean to go through with this crazy deal?"

"Yes."

Épaulard emptied his glass of vodka and shook his head long-sufferingly.

*Followers of the Trotskyist Michel Pablo (Michalis N. Raptis).

"You're a fine bunch of clowns."

"We were a fine bunch of clowns in 1960," said Buenaventura. "And you were one of us."

"Something came out of that."

"Don't make me laugh," cried the Catalan. "You like what it led to? You like Islamic Maoism?"

"Oh shit!" said Épaulard. "Let's not get into theoretical discussions, okay?"

"All right, suit yourself. We're having a meeting tonight. At the place of this guy called Treuffais. I'll leave you his address."

"I guarantee you there's no point."

"I'm leaving it anyway."

Buenaventura took a writing pad and a pencil from the desk and scribbled.

"By the way," he said, "what's all this crap about legal counseling?"

"A job that went south," said Épaulard. "We had a sucker lined up for the classic con about getting hold of the FLN's war booty, the treasure that Khider ripped off. I needed a front. But a couple of weeks ago my partner got himself knocked off in Germany by some Turks, and the mark packed his bags. I was left holding this office, paid up until the end of the month, a 1956 Cadillac, and eyes open."

Buenaventura laughed briefly and poured himself another vodka.

"As a specialist," he said, "we could compensate you."

"With the ambassador's ransom, I suppose?"

"Right."

"You'll never see it."

"What do you know? Come this evening."

"No."

# 6

ALONE now, Épaulard paced nervously up and down his apartment. At one end of the corridor was the office. At the other, his bedroom, containing a bed, a chair, a small table, and a large armoire. On the table were a big legal dictionary intended for heads of families, Roger Vailland's *Écrits intimes* (Personal Diaries), and a few old crime novels, all dog-eared. In the armoire were two pairs of underpants, a set of bed-sheets, six pairs of cotton socks, two neckties in solid colors, two nylon shirts, and a ten-year-old camel-hair overcoat. In the coat's pockets were on one side a box of .30-caliber Mauser ammunition and on the other a Chinese Type 31 automatic. As for the beige raincoat, it lay on the chair.

Épaulard went into the bathroom and examined his face, which the door had struck when Buenaventura burst in. The fifty-year-old bore a pink bruise to the left of his mouth, and his lips were beginning to swell. He nodded his head. He kept looking at his reflection. He had the painful and familiar feeling that he was a failure. He passed his life in review. He was born in the Antilles in the 1920s. At the beginning of the Second World War he was an orphan, penniless, but he owned a boat that took him to South America. The blockade of Norway had created a shortage of cod-liver oil on the world market. Épaulard fished for shark and made a killing with shark-liver oil. Some months later he was in France, and in love. It was for love that he joined the Resistance. An FTP combatant,* he was separated from his unit in a violent skirmish in the Dauphiné in the spring of 1944. By that time he was no longer in love. Having lost his contacts, he made new ones with Gaullist elements and found himself in the Vercors.

After the destruction of the Vercors Maquis, Épaulard, having escaped the massacre, conceived a lively hatred for the bourgeoisie and the Gaullists. He was now a man alone. He became a killer. Between 1945 and 1947 he killed five or six people, out of conviction and for money. Succeeding by luck and good management in remaining unknown to both his clients and to France's police forces, he eventually joined the French Communist Party. There were strikes in the north. Épaulard sabotaged the railroad lines used to deliver armored cars and troops for the purposes of repression. He had a taste of ashes in his mouth. He resolved to assassinate Jules Moch. He abandoned this plan. He was discombobulated. He ran a small print shop in the Paris suburbs. He stopped paying his Party dues.

Beginning in 1957, Épaulard printed all kinds of underground literature produced by left splinter groups opposed to the Communists. Before long he was working for the Algerian National Liberation Front (FLN). He met Buenaventura Diaz, who went by the name of Carlos. He met D'Arcy, already an alcoholic. Leaving France in 1962, he worked with the Pabloists in Algiers on the FLN's program. He quit Algeria after the fall of Ben Bella. He stayed for a short time in Guinea and then landed up in Cuba, working

*FTPF or FTP: Francs-Tireurs et Partisans Français, an armed resistance organization created and led by the French Communist Party.

under Enrique Lister. By this time Épaulard was corrupt. As early as his time in Algeria he had trafficked in abandoned real estate. In Cuba he dabbled in the black market until he was expelled. He traveled in South America before covering his tracks completely. Now here he was, back in France. He had taken the Chinese pistol from his pocket and pressed the barrel to his neck. His finger was on the trigger.

"Might as well end it right now," he told his mirror.

Épaulard sighed and did not finish himself off. He re-pocketed the pistol, a copy of the Russian Tokarev. He consulted his watch. Exactly seven o'clock. He decided he would go to the meeting that night.

"What the hell, why not?" he said to his mirror.

# 7

"THE U.S. Ambassador's schedule is rather inconsistent," Buenaventura reported.

He unfolded a map of Paris on the table and, to make room, Meyer, Treuffais and D'Arcy pushed their just-uncapped bottles of beer aside. As for Épaulard, he remained on his feet, circling the table slowly with his Kronenbourg in one hand and the other hand behind his back, his chin lowered onto his chest and the filter of his Française almost crushed between his lips. From time to time one of the others would cast a furtive glance his way.

"Poindexter is an Episcopalian," Buenaventura went on, "and he attends the eight o'clock service every Sunday morning at the cathedral on Avenue George V. He never sleeps in his official quarters at the embassy; instead he returns every night, though at no particular time, to his residence not far from the Chaillot Cinémathèque. Anywhere from eleven to four in the morning. He goes irregularly to visit the American Hospital in Neuilly. Three times over the past two months while we've been watching him."

As he spoke, the Catalan would point to the spots on the map that the diplomat frequented. He also mentioned a few more locations, all of which the ambassador visited only occasionally.

"All the same," added Buenaventura, "in one way he is as

regular as clockwork. Every week on Friday he spends the evening at a club on the corner of Avenue Kléber and Rue Robert-Soulat."

"Would you be so good as to repeat that?" asked Épaulard, coming to a stop.

Buenaventura wondered why the ex-FTP fighter was suddenly speaking so formally, but he repeated, "Ambassador Poindexter spends every Friday evening at a private club on the corner of Avenue Kléber and Rue Robert-Soulat."

"That's a brothel," declared Épaulard.

"What do you mean?"

"A house of assignation. One of the finest in Paris. The clean and expensive kind."

"Shit!" chuckled D'Arcy. "Another gap in the achievements of the Popular Front!"

"It is the closest whorehouse to the residence of the President of the Republic," went on Épaulard. "Protected by the police, naturally. And it gets very top security whenever some African head of state comes calling."

"Wonderful!" said Buenaventura.

The others looked at him.

"I mean the scandal," said the Catalan. "His Excellency kidnapped by leftists in a whorehouse! *Le Canard Enchainé* will have a field day."

Everyone was delighted. Even Épaulard smiled. Then he bethought himself.

"True, it's as fine a prospect as a dead priest," he acknowledged. "But just the same we have to consider the other possibilities."

"His schedule is inconsistent," Buenaventura recalled.

"We could snatch him at the church service," said D'Arcy.

"Or at home," suggested Meyer. "At night."

"At his residence," said Épaulard, "we might run into anything. FBI guys or you name it, all over the ground floor, for example. A priori, we should reject that. The Protestant service is dangerous because there would be easily a hundred people there. To keep them all quiet you'd need a shitload of people plus machine guns."

"So it's the brothel," said Buenaventura jubilantly.

"We'll have to see," said Épaulard.

Everyone exchanged glances, except for Treuffais, who studied his fingernails.

The former Resistance fighter went over to an armchair and sat down.

"How did you manage to get hold of his schedule?"

"Discreet tailing," said D'Arcy.

"Discreet? This guy must be covered nearly all the time by the French security services and continually surrounded by his own bodyguards. How can you fellows be sure you were discreet enough?"

"We can't. But we took maximum precautions. We used Treuffais's 2CV, which doesn't stand out, and kept our distance. And no RG guys came and asked for the time."*

Épaulard turned to Treuffais.

"No unexpected man from the gas company? No insistent vendors?"

"No."

Épaulard rubbed the side of his nose. He scrutinized each of those present in turn.

"I would like to know your pedigrees," he said. "Whether you have records, and, if so, when and why."

---

*Renseignements Généraux (RG): the domestic intelligence service of the French police until 2008.

He looked directly at Buenaventura.

"D'Arcy and you must have had pretty thick files on you in FLN days. Any problems since?"

Buenaventura shrugged.

"Picked up twice in '68. In Paris and in Flins. To Beaujon for questioning both times."

"Nothing for me," stated the alcoholic.

Épaulard checked the others. Treuffais had never had any contact with the police. Nor had Meyer.

"It all seems pretty clean," Épaulard concluded.

# 8

ON MONDAY morning the awful Ducatel had failed to prepare his presentation on Gabriel Marcel.

"I didn't have the time, sir," he explained.

He sneered soundlessly, revealing yellowed irregular teeth like a dog's. Treuffais gazed at him. Resistance was useless. The lucre of this degenerate was considerable, and good for the taking by Saint-Ange Academy. The imbecile was invulnerable.

"For Friday then, my young friend," said Treuffais.

Then he rose from his chair and began his lesson on modern-day rationalism and its variants. He almost fell asleep three times. At last the clock struck ten. Outside a nasty rain was falling. Treuffais went by the staff room to get his raincoat, which had been hanging up there since the middle of the previous week. Mademoiselle Kugelmann was already correcting papers. Monsieur Duveau was standing near the door with his hands in the pockets of his pinstripe jacket, his bald pate glistening, his pants uncreased, and wine on his breath. He was rocking on his heels and gazing at the drenched windowpanes and the droplets dancing across them.

"Rotten weather," he said to Treuffais.

The young teacher slipped on his raincoat, a great khaki oilskin thing that crackled and retained odors.

"Rotten times too," added Duveau. "Coming for a coffee?"

Mechanically, Treuffais consulted his Kelton and quickly shook his head.

"I'm going home," he replied, feeling the need to clarify. "I don't start again until two."

"You would do better to come for coffee. And a chat. You call yourself a philosophy teacher?" Duveau was mumbling in irritation. "What do you know about life, at your age, I ask you?"

He reached out and grabbed the lapels of Treuffais's raincoat.

"You're pathetic," said Treuffais, and frantically punched the man in the throat.

Duveau gave a great cry and fell down. Electrified, Mademoiselle Kugelmann leapt forward screaming. She rushed to Duveau's side and helped him sit up on the floor. Treuffais was taken aback. He rubbed his knuckles thoughtfully.

"I'm sorry. I didn't want ... I didn't mean ..."

But laughter got the better of him.

"Criminal! Criminal!" cried Duveau feebly.

"For heaven's sake!" shouted Mademoiselle Kugelmann. "What happened? What has gotten into you? Have you no sense? A disabled veteran too! Monsieur Lamour is going to know all about this."

"Monsieur Lamour knows nothing at all," declared Treuffais. "He has shit for brains."

"I heard that, Treuffais," said Monsieur Lamour, who had just silently entered the room.

"Monsieur Lamour, fuck your face!"

"You're out of your mind!"

"I'll beat the crap out of you!"

Red in the face, Monsieur Lamour leant back. He was a

small man. Treuffais could have eaten his supper using the man's head for a table. What a repellent idea! The young philosophy teacher came close to his hierarchical superior, wondering where to hit him. The director remained rigid and solemn, careful not to retreat under the widening eyes of Mademoiselle Kugelmann. Duveau had let himself fall back full-length on the floor so as not to get involved in the fight; he was pretending to be short of breath. Treuffais delivered a tiny slap to the director's livid cheek, walked around the man and left the room, slamming the door behind him.

"I always knew it, but I wanted to give him a chance," declared Monsieur Lamour as he wiped the lenses of his glasses, fogged up from terror. "That fellow is worse than worthless," he concluded. "A complete cipher."

Outside, Treuffais had got into his 2CV. As he slammed the door, his fingers were caught for the umpteenth time by the window, and he swore. He looked at his watch. Eight minutes past ten. He started the car. The 2CV made for Porte d'Orléans. Once in Paris, it turned east at Denfert-Rochereau, crossed the intersection at Les Gobelins, and found a parking spot not far from the university buildings but out of sight of the hordes of cops stationed outside them with their submachine guns hooked to their shoulder straps and their riot helmets dangling at their thighs.

In a brasserie on Boulevard Saint-Marcel, Buenaventura and Épaulard were waiting at the bar with two muscadets in front of them. Treuffais joined them. The rain had stopped.

"Same thing," said the philosophy teacher to the bartender.

"Ten forty," said Épaulard. "We've just been and had a look. A group is dropped off every thirty minutes on the hour and the half hour. We'd better wait for the eleven o'clock. Did you bring the lab coats?"

Inside the first one, Épaulard opened the case holding the cop's automatic pistol and took out a Manurhin PP (Walther licensed), which he pocketed; then he placed the lead bar in the case and closed it. With the familiar weight at his belt, the policeman would probably take a while to realize that his pistol was gone, perhaps not even until he went off duty. Épaulard came out of the cubicle, carefully half closing the latch and holding it thus with his blade until he could slip it out and let the latch fall back into place.

At the next changing room Buenaventura followed exactly the same procedure.

Upon opening the third door, Treuffais found himself face-to-face with a red-faced policeman wearing boxers and a single sock, holding the other sock in his hand, and staring at him in stupefaction.

"Oh, excuse me, I'm looking for Doctor Moreau," said Treuffais with a smile, quickly closing the door, moving away and passing four other doors. He could see Épaulard at the end of the row entering another cubicle. Treuffais was dripping with sweat. He tried another door. There was no one inside. The young teacher grabbed a pistol and got out. Épaulard was striding towards him. Buenaventura had also just exited, and the three men reassembled.

"I've got one," whispered Treuffais.

"Me too," said the Catalan.

"Which makes four. That'll do," said Épaulard. "See you in the street." Treuffais was now drenched in sweat. He consulted his watch: six minutes past eleven.

"Phew!" he said.

"Quick! Quick! To the car!" urged Épaulard.

The sidewalk of the boulevard was crawling with cops. Épaulard and the two anarchists crossed the street.

"A piece of cake," said Buenaventura. "We could easily have taken their ammo too."

"Ammo won't be a problem," said Épaulard.

He kept up the pace all the way to Rue des Plantes, where the Cadillac was parked. As they walked they took off their lab coats and folded them up. When they got to the white car, they placed the firearms inside the folded garments and stowed them beneath the front seats.

"We'll drop you at your 2CV," said Buenaventura to his friend. "We are going to eat in Couzy. Épaulard will be checking the hideout. So we won't have time to take you to your two-o'clock class."

"That doesn't matter now," said Treuffais. "I just lost my job. I won't be holding any more classes."

"What happened?"

"Nothing special. But I'm going to be short of money."

"That's a problem."

"Who cares?" answered Treuffais coldly. "After all, we'll all be rich after this operation, won't we?"

The Catalan shot him a surprised glance.

"We'll sort that out later," said Épaulard impatiently, and started the car.

"Fine," said Buenaventura. "So, in that case, are you coming with us to Couzy?"

"All things considered, no. Drop me at my 2CV."

The Cadillac negotiated narrow streets with relative ease and pulled up briefly by Treuffais's car. The philosophy teacher jumped out, slammed the Cadillac's door, waved goodbye. The Cadillac moved off.

"He's strange, your buddy," said Épaulard.

"He's a troubled soul. He asks himself questions."

The Catalan chuckled.

Treuffais had got into his car. He started it up and headed for his place. When a red light at Rue Alésia turned to green, he trod too brutally on the accelerator, and its return spring snapped. The pedal stuck firmly to the metal beneath Treuffais's foot. Roaring, the car crossed the intersection at top speed in first gear. Treuffais declutched. The engine went on revving to the maximum, and the gas pedal remained stuck. Treuffais steered the vehicle towards a pedestrian crossing, turned off the ignition, and the car bumped the curb gently and came to a halt. The young man got out, opened the hood and surveyed the damage. There was a book and stationery store fifty meters away. Treuffais made his way there. A wooden sign urged "Be Like Everyone—Read *France-Soir.*" Treuffais cleared his throat and directed a gob of mucus onto the stack of newspapers. Entering the store, he bought a rubber band intended for bulky folders, then returned to his car and used the broad, thick elastic as a stand-in for the broken return spring. He set off again, and the 2CV ran as well as before, except that the accelerator was now very loose. Treuffais reached his neighborhood, circled for a while without finding a spot in the busy streets, but finally parked on Rue des Morillons.

He went upstairs. It was five past noon. No mail. He opened a Kronenbourg and sat down in his father's armchair. He pulled a transistor radio towards him and pressed a button.

"Work has resumed following a secret ballot," came the Europe 1 broadcast. "At the Gouraud plant, however, conflict continues. A delegation of unionists was invited this morning to the Ministry of Labor, where they made their case to Monsieur Lhareng. In racing news, there were eighteen horses at the starting gate at Longchamp this afternoon..."

Treuffais turned the radio off. He felt deeply uneasy. He wondered why. Liver trouble? But he finished his beer before leaving his apartment once more to go and eat lunch in a nearby restaurant. After eating he felt no better. His anxiety, he decided, must have a mental origin. He went back home and, raging now, went to bed in his room and tried to go to sleep.

# 9

THE CADILLAC jolted horribly on the dirt road and threw up clods of cold mud that streaked its sides. It followed the badly maintained byroad, classified as "rural," before stopping with its nose against a barrier. This was a primitive structure—a few stakes linked by barbed wire and flanked by two gateposts. Buenaventura got out of the car and opened it, rolling the wire up and placing it by one of the posts. The Cadillac entered an area covered with gray and yellow grass that surrounded a farm.

The landscape was hill and dale, woodland and pasture. The loamy soil was sodden. On hilltops and in hollows leafless trees could be seen, black against the darkish green of the grass, gray against the gray sky.

The farmstead was on the flat, shaped like a right-angled letter U. Two short wings stood perpendicular to the main house, roughcasted and roofed in brown tile. There was an attic story. The left-hand wing was just a garage, the right-hand one old unrestored stables. The whole place was fairly small. Its isolation was startling in a region of clustered hamlets and small towns. In view of its age, it would have been of interest to ethnologists or geographers specializing in human settlement. Buenaventura and Épaulard couldn't have cared less. The Cadillac had pulled up between the two wings. Buenaventura had reclosed the barrier, and now the two men approached the front of the house and its glazed door. The Catalan tapped on the glass. No reply. He tried the handle, and the door opened. The pair entered a living area with a tiled floor, a gigantic table, a great fireplace with a metal hood, and a staircase that disappeared towards the upper floor.

"Cash?" called Buenaventura.

No response. Hands in the pockets of his damp raincoat, Épaulard walked around the room, which measured some fifty square meters and had three large windows with small panes and wooden shutters, a bench, four chairs, and two caved-in upholstered armchairs by the fireside. Beneath the staircase, which climbed obliquely up the back wall, were two doors, one leading to a kitchen, the other out to the rear of the farmhouse. The latter opened at that very moment to reveal an apparition. Épaulard raised an eyebrow, for it simply did not make sense: Why was a girl like this involved in such a crummy operation? For she was beautiful, but more than that: she was put together. Light blond hair falling to her shoulders, a delightful nose à la Hedy Lamarr, brownish-green eyes, high cheekbones. Her makeup was of British inspiration (looking at her, Épaulard smiled automatically); she had put rouge on her cheeks before powdering them lightly, her lips were red, her body was ecstatically small, and she was wearing black cotton pants and a shimmering loose shirt with loud vertical stripes, red, pink, orange, and white.

Buenaventura slipped past Épaulard and kissed her on either cheek.

"Hi, Cash."

"And you, sir?" Cash asked Épaulard.

The fifty-year-old stuck a Française in his mouth and his lips crushed the filter. He searched his pockets for matches.

"André Épaulard," said Buenaventura.

"Hi," said Cash.

She took Épaulard's mitt. Her hand was small but her shake was strong.

"He's in with us on the job," said the Catalan.

"The job?"

"The ambassador."

Cash raised her reshaped eyebrows.

"I wasn't expecting you. I have nothing to eat here."

"We stopped in Couzy. We have rib steaks and potatoes. In the car. Can we put it in the garage?"

"Of course."

The Catalan looked inquiringly at Épaulard, who took the car keys from his raincoat pocket and held them out.

"Good, I'll get the chow," said Buenaventura, taking the keys and leaving through the glazed door.

Épaulard lit his cigarette. Cash looked at him through the smoke.

"Would you like a drink? Scotch?"

"Yes, I would."

The sometime maquisard sat down on the bench alongside the enormous table. Cash opened a dark sideboard and brought out three glasses and a bottle of Johnnie Walker Red Label, three-quarters full, with a little Prisunic stamp on its soft-metal screw top.

"I'll get some ice."

She went out through the communicating door, leaving it ajar. Épaulard glimpsed a kitchen with many Formica-covered cabinets. The girl rummaged in a large refrigerator and came back with ice cubes and a magnum of Perrier. She poured Scotch into the three glasses, adding two ice cubes to each, and then sat down opposite Épaulard. He contemplated her and found her exciting. He was excited.

"You look like Roger Vailland," observed Cash.

To Épaulard's mind this felt like a cold shower. I am an unanalyzable person, his ego claimed silently, not a personality (his id just said "Meh"). Not so easy, though, to make that claim with a mug like mine, and with my résumé: militant turned crook, former killer—yes, I've lived, I'm way past fifty. And for eighteen months he hadn't so much as touched a girl and, what was worse, had not even felt the need until now. He recalled an inventive Cuban prostitute and blushed stupidly. He stabbed his Française furiously into a white and gold Martini ashtray, rubbing it on the bottom to make sure it was out, then produced another cigarette and lit it immediately.

"No literature, if you don't mind."

"Don't you like Roger Vailland?"

"Well, yes, a little."

"Have you met him?"

"No. Let's talk about something else, if you don't mind. Literature is of no interest."

"I'm a character like the young bourgeois girl in *Playing with Fire*," persisted Cash.

"What the fuck do I care? Or do you want me to pop your cherry?" asked Épaulard in a spasm of vulgarity. "You know, you're beginning to worry me," he added. "I have no desire to work with clowns on a thing like . . . a thing like what we're here for."

"Okay, okay."

"Why don't you show me the layout instead," said Épaulard, getting to his feet with his glass in his hand and his cigarette in his mouth.

Cash acquiesced. The small door beneath the staircase through which she had entered the room gave onto several hectares of grassy orchard. Hutches lined the back wall of the farmhouse. Inside them rabbits were busy nibbling.

"I was in the middle of feeding them when you arrived," said Cash. "But don't get me wrong. Boring, easy tasks are not my thing. I don't know what my style is. I'm nothing but a little whore."

Chatter away, thought Épaulard. The former FTPer checked the lay of the land. Plenty of trees meant good cover in the event of incoming gunfire. But what in hell am I thinking? he asked himself. We are not here to face a siege. If we're going to get to that point, we might as well surrender right now. We'd be completely screwed. He went back into the common area of the farmhouse. Buenaventura, after garaging the Cadillac, had just returned with two string bags containing the steaks and potatoes.

"I'm getting the tour," said Épaulard.

"Carry on. I'll light the fire."

The Catalan took a hit of Scotch and went over to the fireplace. He began laying crumpled newspaper between the andirons and breaking up kindling. Cash showed Épaulard the kitchen: a window overlooking the rear of the house; a connecting door to a disused workshop festooned with cobwebs.

The girl closed the workshop door, returned to the common area and approached the foot of the staircase. Épaulard followed her. As they climbed the stairs, he looked at her ass, which was magnificently small and as muscular as that of a young boxer dog. At the top of the stairs was a landing and a long corridor with four doors and very narrow windows like arrow slits overlooking the back of the house.

"A bathroom and three bedrooms," said Cash.

Épaulard glanced into the bathroom, which received

natural light via large frosted-glass blocks, then he inspected each bedroom in turn; they were rather similar with their white walls, two small dormer windows in each, a double bed in one and twin beds in the other two, shelves and chests of drawers here and there. The fifty-year-old absentmindedly picked up a grubby and creased paperback lying on the floor whose subject was "the Maoist movement in France."

"Don't tell me you're a Maoist?"

"I'm not a complete idiot," answered Cash.

Épaulard tossed the book onto a bed and went out into the half darkness of the passage, which smelled of sap or perhaps wax. Cash closed the door behind him and pushed him in a friendly way towards the staircase.

"That's all there is to see. The ambassador, in my opinion, should be put in one of the rooms with twin beds, with one of you there to keep an eye on him. I'll keep the one with the double bed, which is my room. That'll leave two beds for four people. But anyway I expect that someone will have to be on watch downstairs, so it might as well be two—they can play cards."

"Won't one of us be your lover?" asked Épaulard idly as he went down the stairs.

"Neither one nor any of you. Should I show you the garage and the barn or should we have lunch?"

"It's not ready yet," said Buenaventura, who had overheard them now that Épaulard and the girl had reached the foot of the stairs.

"We'll take a look later," said Épaulard. "Let's relax and have that drink."

He was still holding his Scotch. He emptied the glass, poured himself another, stubbed out his cigarette and lit another, coughed violently, and sat down. Buenaventura poked the fire, shifting the already-glowing logs. He slipped potatoes among the embers and covered them with ash, then he unwrapped the steaks and placed them in a long-handled grilling basket.

"For the steak," he said, "I'll wait a bit. It'll take a good twenty or twenty-five minutes for the potatoes to be done."

After setting the caged steaks down near the fire, he went back to the end of the table and took another sip of whiskey.

"This place work for you?" he asked Épaulard.

"Yes."

"Of course you'll still want to study maps and all that. Want to see the map?"

"That can wait."

"Is something bothering you?"

Épaulard burst out laughing.

"What bothers me is the presence of girls."

"I'm not a girl, I'm a whore," said Cash.

"Don't exaggerate, Cash," said the Catalan.

"I'm a kept woman. This house for instance. You can bless the trick who lent it to me while he's spending the winter in the United States to work on his marketing skills, racketeering skills. Pubic relations, more like."

"And she didn't even let him screw her," Buenaventura scoffed.

"Not true," said Cash.

"You kept that from me."

"I did," said Cash. "But I wouldn't want it to be thought that I was unavailable." She looked coolly at Épaulard.

The fifty-year-old did not know what to think. His mind chose the easiest answer and he told himself that the girl was a slut, that he would poke her when he wanted, where he wanted, in a hayloft if he wanted. He emptied his glass and looked down at the wooden tabletop.

"May we know why you let yourself get mixed up in a setup like the one we have in mind?"

Cash pouted sardonically.

"I believe in universal harmony," she said, "and in the destruction of the pitiful civilized State. My cool and chic exterior hides the wild flames of a burning hatred for a techno-bureaucratic capitalism whose cunt looks like a funeral urn and whose mug looks like a prick. Should I go on?"

Épaulard gazed at her bug-eyed.

"Don't get bent out of shape, comrade," said Buenaventura. "She is the great inscrutable, this chick."

# 10

TREUFFAIS woke up to the telephone ringing. He got out of bed and picked up the receiver.

"Marcel Treuffais here."

"Buenaventura Diaz."

"Where are you?"

"We're back. At my friend's now. He thought everything was hunky-dory. He's going to try and solve the transport question, and if that works out pronto, we can think in terms of Friday."

"This Friday!"

"Well, what do you think? Why not?"

"We haven't—well, yes, yes, okay," said Treuffais, pushing hair away from his eyes.

"We meet tomorrow evening at your place. Let the others know."

"Okay."

"So long then. André and I still have a lot of things to take care of."

"Good."

The Catalan hung up and turned to Épaulard, who was sitting at his fake legal counsel's desk. He had cleared it off completely and spread one of the lab coats over it as a sheet on which to disassemble their automatic weapons, whose working order he was now checking.

48

"He's a strange one, your Treuffais, it seems to me," said Buenaventura.

Épaulard looked up.

"Is he scared?"

"I don't know. But that's not the problem. You're going to laugh at this, but I'm not sure he is quite with us, politically."

"Why would I laugh?"

"You yourself aren't really on board politically either," said Buenaventura. "But you are up for it anyway. It's what I was saying about despair."

"Don't fuck with me, boy. Can we bank on Treuffais, yes or no?"

"He's my friend."

"That's not what I asked you."

"It's my answer."

"If it's like that, we'll do the job just the four of us."

"You're joking."

"Not in the least."

"But Treuffais is with us!" protested Buenaventura. "He wrote most of our manifesto. He…no, no…well, fuck it, you can't be serious."

The Catalan had begun striding up and down the office, his black hair flopping over his eyes and his teeth bared by a grimace of agitation. He dropped into a leather armchair. Just then the phone rang. Épaulard picked up.

"Épaulard Legal Counsel Offices," he announced, then he listened, pursed his lips, and passed the receiver to Buenaventura. "It's for you," he said. "Treuffais."

"Hello."

"Buen? I have to see you."

"Why?"

"I must talk to you. Privately, please."

"This evening then. Will you come to me?"

"At your hotel? Yes, if you like. What time?"

"Eight o'clock?"

"Fine. We'll go for dinner together maybe."

"Oh, just 'maybe'?" said Buenaventura. "That bad, huh? Anyway, eight o'clock it is."

"Bye."

The Catalan did not reply. Treuffais stayed on the line. Buenaventura could hear him breathing.

"Hello? Are you there?" went the phone.

Buenaventura rang off. Épaulard was looking at him knowingly.

"He's copping out?"

"I have no idea. Maybe. I'll see him a bit later."

"All right," said Épaulard. "We'll talk about it again tomorrow. I'm off. Must go to Ivry to see about ammo and transport. If your pal pulls out, perhaps you'll contact Meyer and D'Arcy to let them know that we'll be meeting here tomorrow."

Quickly, the fifty-year-old finished reassembling the automatics, wrapped them up again in the lab coats and made a kind of bundle of all of them that he put away in the khaki metal cabinet. Each man tossed down a vodka, left the office, and went his separate way.

# 11

THAT SAME evening (Monday), Épaulard bartered his Cadillac in Ivry for two hundred and fifty .32 ACP cartridges, which the Manurhins would swallow with ease; the promise of his picking up, on Friday at 2:00 p.m., a completely decrepit old green Jaguar with another few hundred kilometers in it for sure; and a registration card that was not obviously fake. Being a practical man, Épaulard demanded some extra cans of oil and, seeing that the hand brake was of course quite useless, made a mental note to get a wooden chock in case he had to park on a hill. His visit to Ivry and his negotiations there gave him the opportunity to eat an excellent meal in a cheap local café and to chat about the good old days with the Gypsy who had haggled with him over the Jaguar. They recalled the Mediterranean, and the shoot-outs with SFIO pistoleros and ex-Gestapo men infiltrated into the DGER, with not a few dead but quite a few survivors.* Épaulard went home seriously drunk and in rather good spirits.

Meanwhile, Buenaventura and Treuffais were meeting in the Catalan's room. Treuffais stated that he did not intend

---

*SFIO: Section Française de l'Internationale Ouvrière (1905–1969), forerunner of France's Socialist Party; DGER: Direction Générale des Études et Recherches, Free French intelligence service.

to take part in the operation and gave his reasons. The upshot was a rather short but bitter and distressing conversation, and the two friends did not eat dinner together. Later that evening Buenaventura informed D'Arcy that they would meet the next day at Épaulard's and asked him to let Meyer, who had no telephone, know about this.

On Tuesday morning Buenaventura joined Épaulard at his place and apprised him of Treuffais's defection. He explained that the disagreement was theoretical in nature and that therefore there was nothing to fear from Treuffais, who was a friend and could not be suspected of being in touch with the police and would keep his mouth shut.

"I don't like it," declared Épaulard.

"I can vouch for Treuffais's loyalty," said Buenaventura somewhat stiffly. "I have as much confidence in him as in you."

Épaulard reflected for a moment.

"Okay."

On Tuesday night, Meyer, D'Arcy, Buenaventura and Épaulard met in Épaulard's office. Meyer and D'Arcy were told that Treuffais had dropped out. Meyer made no comment. D'Arcy commented in obscene terms but added that he couldn't give a shit. Both agreed with the Catalan that this defection did not worsen the risks.

Then, so far as possible, they decided on the order of events during the kidnapping of Ambassador Poindexter and the days following.

It may be noted that at the same moment the aforesaid Poindexter was attending a performance of *Tristan and Isolde* after going to a reception in the function rooms of Hôtel George V. The ambassador was a tall man with a pointy balding head and watery blue eyes behind gold-rimmed eyeglasses. He wore an expression of perpetual mild surprise, distinct interest, and congenial amusement. Wagner's music brought a slight change in this attitude: interest won out over surprise and amusement disappeared. All of it was carefully measured. The ambassador's wife was by his side, very tall with a scrawny neck and horsey teeth—beautiful and classy, no doubt, in the eyes of her uptight peers. She was very bored all the time, but had not noticed it for over forty years. They made a handsome couple. They had separate bedrooms. They did number two once a day. Apart from them their box was empty, but outside the door stood two cops—blond, young, resolute, muscled, trained by the FBI and the NSA; two more sat in a Citroën DS21 parked not far from the Opéra, while a third, in a chauffeur's uniform, was smoking a Pall Mall by the official Lincoln.

In Épaulard's office, Buenaventura was passing around photos of Poindexter clipped from American magazines, some of them in color. Before long the meeting came to an end.

On the Wednesday the terrorists stayed in. Except for Véronique Cash, who got her rusty Renault Dauphine out of the farmhouse garage and began her shopping. She would buy a six-pack of beer and two boxes of pasta at one place, five kilos of potatoes and ham at another, wine and canned meat at yet another, other things elsewhere again, and so on. She returned to the farmhouse between trips to unload. Perishables piled up in the fridge, and other items went into the old stables.

On the Thursday nobody did anything. Treuffais lay in his bedroom smoking nonstop; the room stank of cold tobacco smoke, warm tobacco smoke, and dirty feet. The young man had three days' worth of stubble. He bit his nails. He tried in vain to read. He got up once to call Buenaventura on the phone but hung up before he finished dialing the number of the Longuevache Hotel.

On the Friday, the anarcho-terrorist squad kidnapped the U.S. Ambassador.

# 12

In ivry, at 2:00 p.m., Épaulard took possession of the green Jaguar and the paperwork. The machine dated from 1954. Its suspension was a horror, and acid escaping from successive batteries had made holes in the partition between the engine bay and the interior of the car. A wintry draft chilled Épaulard's knees. He drove back into Paris and met his companions at Place d'Italie. Everyone got into the car. Épaulard gave the wheel to D'Arcy. The alcoholic's hands were trembling. Once they gripped the wheel, they steadied. The automobile set off gently back to Porte d'Italie. D'Arcy familiarized himself with its operation. The four men smoked continually and left their cigarette butts on the car floor. D'Arcy took the Autoroute du Sud, getting bolder and pushing the motor to the limit. Just before reaching 120 kph it began to hesitate and judder. D'Arcy groaned, grasped the wheel ever more tightly and accelerated once more, but the vibration reached fever pitch and the Jaguar's rear end swayed from side to side more impressively than Sophia Loren's. The driver raised his foot, dropped back down to 100 kph, and wiped his brow with his sleeve.

"That bastard Pepito," grumbled Épaulard. "He swore she would get up to 140."

"On the roads we are taking," said D'Arcy, "there would be no chance of that anyway. This will do."

He got off the highway at Longjumeau and headed back towards Paris via all kinds of minor roads and side streets, testing the car's performance on bends, while braking, and over cobblestones. Eventually they reentered Paris by way of the Porte d'Orléans.

"Twenty to five," noted Épaulard. "Let's step on it and beat the traffic jams."

At five in the afternoon the Jaguar was parked dutifully on the third level down of the Champs-Élysées/George V underground garage. The men closed the doors, took the elevator to the exit and the Métro to Concorde, then repaired to Épaulard's to wait.

"Your place is handy," remarked D'Arcy. "Just a stone's throw from the embassy."

They settled down in the kitchen to play Fuck Your Buddy with kitchen matches for chips. As time went on, the players became more nervous. D'Arcy and Meyer ended up leaving the table and retreating to Épaulard's bedroom. The alcoholic stayed still, silent, smoking and doing nothing, his hands shaking, while Meyer stretched out on the bed, leant on his side and tried to read Jonathan Latimer's *The Dead Don't Care*, a not very reassuring title. Épaulard and the Catalan stayed in the office playing Sinking Sands, a nasty stud poker variation in which the first card a player turns faceup is wild along with others of the same rank in their hand. Buenaventura won every time.

"You're overdoing it," Épaulard complained.

"Poker is my bread and butter," retorted the Catalan. "My only honest income."

"You call it honest!"

Buenaventura chortled.

"What are you whining about? We're not playing for dough."

D'Arcy came out of the bedroom.

"It's seven o'clock. Perhaps we could go for a bite?"

"If you want an expert opinion," said Épaulard, "we shouldn't go for a bite. The trick is to have an empty stomach in case of a gut shot."

"A real optimist, this guy," said D'Arcy.

"Three jacks."

"Shit!"

The Catalan raked in his matches. Seeing that nobody was paying attention to him anymore, D'Arcy went back into the bedroom grumbling. A little later eight o'clock came around, and Épaulard announced that it was time to go to work. D'Arcy left the building carrying a screwdriver with a set of interchangeable heads. He stopped at the end of the street to toss down a double Ricard in a dive, then walked on to Place de la Concorde and thence towards Place de l'Étoile. He inspected the parked cars. Not far from the Petit Palais, he came upon a Consul station wagon with an open window. He got into the vehicle and spent a good ten minutes hot-wiring it and unlocking the steering wheel. He set the car in motion, merged into the still fairly heavy traffic, made a detour so as to get onto Rue de Rivoli westbound, found a parking space, popped in for another double Ricard, and went back up to Épaulard's.

"Haul ass," he urged. "I'm on a taxi rank."

"Stupid idiot!" said Épaulard, handing him an automatic, which the alcoholic pocketed.

The others were all ready to go, shooters in their pockets and sneakers on their feet—except for Épaulard, who wore leather shoes—and sweaters and jackets for everyone. They went briskly downstairs, reached Rue de Rivoli shivering in the cold air, got into the Consul and turned off towards Place de l'Étoile.

Ten past nine.

From Place de l'Étoile, where the traffic was flowing and a light drizzle was falling, the Consul started down Avenue Kléber. Épaulard counted the traffic lights.

"Next right."

"I know," said D'Arcy.

Screwing up his eyes, Épaulard scanned the cars parked by the sidewalks.

"It's here. Stop!"

The Consul crossed the intersection, put its blinkers on, and halted on a pedestrian crosswalk. Épaulard and Buenaventura got out.

"In five minutes exactly, Meyer goes in," said Épaulard. "Five minutes after that you double-park the car in front of the cathouse."

"We know," said D'Arcy.

The car door slammed. The Consul set off on a quick circuit that would bring it back to the same place in a few minutes. Épaulard and the Catalan headed down the street with the brothel. At the top of three steps an outer door of varnished brown wood had a Judas window. Tiny gilt metal letters, almost indecipherable, spelled out CLUB ZERO. Épaulard rang briefly and waited.

Fifty meters away, in the Triumph Dolomite which Ambassador Poindexter used for his weekly escapade and which was parked legally by the sidewalk, Agent Bunker left off his reading of *Ramparts* magazine to scrutinize the two men waiting to be admitted at the entrance to the brothel. He noticed that one of them was wearing sneakers. With an elbow he nudged Agent Lewis, who was snoozing next to him, and with his chin he indicated the objects of his curiosity.

"A gray-haired Romeo and a little faggot," hazarded Agent Lewis.

The Judas hole opened to reveal the face of a well-coiffed, dark-skinned young woman with heavily made-up eyes and pursed lips.

"Gentlemen?"

"I haven't been here for a very long time," murmured Épaulard urbanely. "We don't know each other and I daresay you would be disinclined to admit me on the sole basis of my honest face. I am not a member of the club but I come recommended by friends whose names will be recognized by Madame Gabrielle."

By way of an example, he gave the childish nickname used by a senator who had patronized the establishment in the 1950s.

"Just a moment, if you don't mind, sir," said the dark-skinned woman, and the Judas window closed.

Épaulard looked at his watch. Fifty seconds had elapsed. Thirty more went by and then the door opened. A lady in a Chanel pantsuit stood on the threshold with the dark-skinned woman a few steps behind her. Behind the two of them hung closed drapes.

"Your face says nothing to me," said Madame Gabrielle. "But if you know Bichon . . . may I invite you to join us at the bar, sir?"

"Lucas," said Épaulard. "And this is Georges, my protégé." Buenaventura kissed the lady's hand. She was moderately charmed.

"Very well then, fine," she said. "Come on in."

They parted the drapes and went through into a faux Louis XV lobby from which a twisting staircase led upwards. Madame Gabrielle steered the two newcomers through a door on the ground floor into a dimly lit bar, likewise Louis XV, with lilies in vases and a red telephone on the counter. Behind the latter stood a burly bartender in a white jacket with beyond-incipient male-pattern baldness and a bushy mustache. He resembled the saxophonist Guy Lafitte. Perched on a barstool was a tall young man, with fair hair *en brosse* and a Chartreuse in front of him, reading *The Greening of America* in a paperback edition. Two minutes had passed since the two got out of the Consul. Madame Gabrielle sized up the Catalan. His scruffiness made her wary.

"I'm sure you appreciate my protégé's simplicity," murmured Épaulard. "His rough-and-readiness, so to speak."

The madam shot him a sideways glance. Here was a true man of the world. She relaxed.

"The first round is on me," she said, and she was preparing to step behind the bar when Agent Ricardo looked up discreetly from his paperback to scrutinize the new arrivals and, noticing Buenaventura's bulging pocket, immediately concluded that the young man was armed and reached into his own jacket.

Épaulard grabbed a barstool by one of its legs and brandished it. Agent Ricardo fired through his pocket. The round buried itself in the ceiling, and the report, muffled by the material of his jacket, might have been mistaken for the popping of a champagne cork. Épaulard pistol-whipped the American, felling him instantly. Simultaneously, Buenaventura had fired his own 7.65, whose barrel was now pointed at the barman.

"Don't try ducking behind the bar," said the Catalan.

"Turn around, place your hands against the bottles, fists clenched. Do not move your fingers."

The barman obeyed. Madame Gabrielle stood completely still.

"There's no money here," she said.

"You are a liar, my dear little lady," Épaulard told her, backing briskly towards the bar entrance, and when the hostess rushed in, attracted by the ruckus, he delivered an uppercut to her jaw, and the girl fell to the floor like a sack of potatoes.

Two and a half minutes had passed.

Épaulard continued to back up, exited the bar, reached for the drapes and tore them down, then came back in. He ripped the material into strips. The dark-skinned girl, Agent Ricardo, and the barman (already laid low by a karate chop to the nape of the neck) were swiftly bound and gagged. Épaulard turned to the madam.

Three and a half minutes.

"How many people are in your palace at this moment?"

The madam made no reply. Épaulard grabbed the knife the barman used to slice lemons and went up to her.

"I'm in a hurry. Answer me, or I'll widen your mouth with this."

"Three clients and three girls," the madam replied quickly. "It's still very early," she explained.

"Are you expecting anyone else?"

"Yes."

"When?"

The madam eyed the knife.

"They'll be here soon. You'd do better to give up, son."

"What room is Ambassador Poindexter in?"

"You came for him? Are you leftists?"

"Shut up! What room?"

"The Blue Room," she sighed.

"And where is it, this Blue Room?"

Four minutes.

"Upstairs. Second door on the right."

"Okay," said Épaulard, picking up what was left of the drapes.

"You won't get away with this," said the madam. "I have protection. Nobody can do this to me and get away with it. You would do better...Oh! Please don't gag me. I'm very nervous and I'm afraid of not being able to breathe."

"Shut up!"

Épaulard tied the woman up, twisting pieces of fabric around her head and knotting them. She groaned unintelligibly.

Five minutes.

Meyer rang the doorbell of the house of assignation. In the Triumph Dolomite, Agent Bunker leant forward.

"Another young guy in tennis shoes," he observed in an urgent tone of voice. "We'd better go and take a look-see. This stinks."

"Oh hell!" swore Agent Lewis distractedly as he started the car.

Up the street, the brothel's front door opened, and Meyer went inside to be greeted by Épaulard.

"You come upstairs with me," said the fifty-year-old. "Buen will stay in the bar to keep an eye."

Directly across the street from the brothel, upstairs at No. 2, a pale-faced felon named Bouboune, a supernumerary of an internal faction within the SDECE,* was bored to

*Service de Documentation Extérieure et de Contre-Espionnage. France's foreign intelligence agency (1944–82).

tears with his Sankyo movie camera and his liter of VDQS Corbières. All the same, he noted with interest that the American Ambassador's Triumph had pulled out and was slowly edging up to the front of Club Zero.

Upstairs inside the bordello, through the second door on the right, Épaulard and Meyer, weapons in hand, silently entered the Blue Room. Ambassador Poindexter was very surprised. He had not yet gone into action. Sitting in an armchair fully dressed, flushed, with a brandy in his hand, he was contemplating his favorite call girl, who was almost completely naked, as she slowly removed her stockings. She was a magnificent milky blonde with hollow cheeks and a broadly contemptuous expression. She stifled a little cry and remained calm, her eyebrows raised. Meyer aimed his automatic at Poindexter.

"Nobody move," ordered Épaulard in a low voice.

He stood behind the girl.

"Don't worry. We are not gangsters or sadists," he murmured. "Just relax. I'm going to knock you out, but it will leave no marks."

Philosophically, the girl relaxed. Épaulard delivered a swift chop to her neck and caught her as she toppled, touching a firm breast with a tinge of pleasure. He laid her down on the bed, tied her up with her clothing, stuffing one stocking in her mouth and slipping the other over her head.

"Have a heart," said Poindexter.

"Can it! We won't hurt you so long as you do what we say. Do you understand French?"

"Yes, yes, of course."

The ambassador was quaking.

"Have a heart," he repeated. "I have a wife."

"Shut up! On your feet! Meyer, you go out ahead of him.

Follow him, you. Come on, get going. Obey and everything will be fine. If you don't, I'll kill you. Get it?"

"Yes. Have a heart."

"Shut up! Go! Faster!"

Eight minutes.

The group reached the ground floor. The front doorbell rang. Épaulard shoved Poindexter into the bar.

"Watch him, Meyer. Rip out the telephone wires. I'm going to open the door. You stay where you are, Buen."

With his automatic in his right hand behind his back, Épaulard went and half opened the front door. Agent Bunker was standing outside. He looked Épaulard up and down.

"Yes, Monsieur?" asked the fifty-year-old.

"Would you mind telling Madame Gabrielle that the American has an extremely important message," said Agent Bunker with a strong American accent.

"With pleasure," answered Épaulard. Over the agent's shoulder he could see the Triumph double-parked, its motor running, and a man at the wheel. "Kindly step inside. You will have to wait for a moment in the bar."

Eight minutes and forty seconds.

D'Arcy was completing his second loop a little early. He pulled up again on the pedestrian crosswalk at the corner of Avenue Kléber. From there he could see the bordello's front door, open, and the man at the top of the steps. He frowned.

"No thank you," said Bunker, taking a step back.

Taking a chance that his gun might go off, Épaulard jabbed the barrel savagely into the agent's solar plexus. The man gave a horrid sigh and fell backwards. Épaulard tried to grab him by the lapels and pull him inside as though nothing had happened, but he did not have time and caught hold of only the man's striped tie. Bunker continued nevertheless to tumble and hung for a moment at the end of his tie, then Épaulard let go and he landed on his back on the sidewalk and lost his hat.

D'Arcy urged the Consul station wagon forward.

The felon Bouboune snatched up his movie camera.

"Come out here! Come out here! Bring him out here!" yelled Épaulard to his companions, for he could see the Consul approaching. At that moment Agent Lewis got out of the Triumph on the roadway side and took aim at the former Resistance fighter with an S&W Bodyguard Airweight. Épaulard opened fire instantly. The Triumph's windshield shattered. Agent Lewis dropped flat onto the street. D'Arcy, instead of stopping, stepped on the gas and ran him over.

"When it comes to discretion, we suck," he observed as he brought the Consul to a halt.

The felon Bouboune had his camera working and was filming the street excitedly.

At the sound of the gunshot, windows overlooking the street opened, two or three of them. And with a great roaring of engines two motorcycle cops burst out from a porte-cochère at the far end of the street and raced down towards the brothel, from which Meyer, Buenaventura and Épaulard were just emerging, dragging with them an ambassador rigid with fear.

"Get the hell out of here!" yelled Épaulard to D'Arcy, for he had decided to give himself up while there was still time, while there were still (he hoped) no fatalities.

"Fuck your mother!" retorted D'Arcy, getting out of the Consul and opening fire on the motorcycle cops.

His first shot went high. The second shattered the shoulder

of the leading cop, who crashed noisily to the ground along with his machine. After that D'Arcy's pistol jammed.

"Oh well, so be it," said Épaulard, taking aim with his own weapon.

"So be it, fire!" added Buenaventura, who was given to quotation, and both men fired at the second cop, who sailed, twirling, from his bike.

At his window the felon Bouboune was filming ever more gleefully.

The second cop's bike bounced back and forth from one side of the street to the other, sideswiping parked cars, until it fell onto its side.

Nine and a half minutes.

The cop with the shattered shoulder was twisting and turning in the middle of the street. The other one lay unconscious on the hood of a Peugeot 404. The one on the ground drew his gun. Meyer and Épaulard were unceremoniously loading the ambassador into the back of the Consul. Standing beside the car, which Buenaventura was darting around on his way to the passenger seat, D'Arcy noticed the contortions of the wounded cop, who seemed set on popping one off. Pocketing his jammed gun, the alcoholic produced a Manufrance catapult with an aluminum frame from his jacket, loaded it with a steel ball bearing and stretched back the rubber sling. It's impossible, thought the motorcycle cop, this guy is aiming at me with a slingshot. Then he heard the rubber violently released and the ball bearing struck the center of his helmet, perforated the helmet, and perforated his skull. The startled motorcycle cop fell flat on his face, dead.

D'Arcy got back into the Consul. Everyone was now in.

"Have a heart! Have a heart!" the ambassador continued to groan. This irritated the kidnappers, but not overmuch.

D'Arcy reversed as fast as he could. Agent Lewis, half-dead under the station wagon, gave a pitiful scream as the front tires ran over him a second time. The car reached the corner and then, shifting into forward gear, swerved off down Avenue Kléber and headed for Place de l'Étoile at a high rate of speed.

"I'm a murderer," said D'Arcy.

"Settle down," said Épaulard. "You ran down an American agent and knocked out a cop. That's all."

"I killed that cop."

"With a slingshot?"

"I killed him," D'Arcy repeated calmly. "I want to drink myself to oblivion."

"No time for that," said Buenaventura.

At a quarter to ten, the Consul entered the Champs-Élysées parking garage. Cars were changed on the third level down. Bound and gagged, with a bag over his head, Ambassador Poindexter was placed in the green Jaguar's trunk. Meanwhile Épaulard carefully wiped down the steering wheel and controls of the Consul along with its door handles. He then joined the others in the Jag, which left the parking garage through the Avenue George V exit. Taking the Right Bank Expressway, the vehicle reached the ring road not many minutes after ten. It left the city via Porte de Bercy only moments before it was closed by the police, who had now been fully alerted and gone into action combing the night streets.

Thereafter things were less unpredictable but more complicated. The suburbs were a labyrinth of streets through which Épaulard had meticulously worked out a route. Beyond Chelles, as they came out into the country, small roads proliferated. Law enforcement was hardly equipped to block them all. Soon after midnight, having taken well over two hours to cover less than sixty kilometers as the crow flies (but almost double that on the odometer), the green Jaguar reached the farmhouse near Couzy just as it began to snow.

# 13

ON FRIDAY, after lunch, the minister of the interior had left for a long weekend at his château in Indre-et-Loire. At ten past ten that night, he was watching a televised debate on abortion with a measure of disgust when he received a telephone call informing him of the abduction of Richard Poindexter. His chief of staff was already summoning representatives of the national police, the army, the gendarmerie, and the police intelligence service (RG) to the ministry on Place Beauvau. He had given the order for the blocking of city streets and highways in accordance with the plan drawn up for dealing with such eventualities. The prime minister, the Élysée Palace, and Foreign Affairs had been alerted. The minister of the interior said that this was all good and called for a helicopter. On the grounds of his château he had the appropriate guidance lights turned on, and it was not long before an SA316 descended from the heavens. At eleven thirty that night the minister was in his ministry, having been apprised in the interim by radio of all developments, of which as of now there were precious few.

At this same time, Marcel Treuffais, very much on edge, had listened to the eleven o'clock news, which made no mention of a kidnapping, and was smoking his last Gauloise before going out to buy more. He went on foot to the Convention intersection, where he found an open *tabac* and bought four packs of cigarettes. As he left the shop, two motorcycle cops went through heading west at full throttle. Treuffais got butterflies in his stomach, then became aware by watching the cops that a barrier had been set up a few hundred meters away where Rue de la Convention met Rue Lecourbe. Turning, he saw that there was another one on Rue de Vaugirard about half a kilometer to the north. His throat tightened, his heart beat faster, and he hurried to get home. Once again he turned on his old Radialva, just in time to hear a communiqué from the Ministry of the Interior that interrupted *Pop Club*: "This evening in Paris, as he was leaving a club where he had dined, Richard Poindexter, the U.S. Ambassador to France, was attacked and abducted by an unknown armed group who fired on the ambassador's entourage." The ambassador's chauffeur had been gravely injured, as had a French police officer, and another police officer had been killed. The government was determined to shine the brightest light on this repellent act and to find its perpetrators in short order so that they might be punished in an exemplary manner and to the full extent of the law. Investigators' initial inquiries made it possible to say that this attack was the work of individuals who, whether by virtue of insanity or of calculation, were resolved to create disorder at any cost. They should expect no weakness on the part of the State, nor the slightest clemency unless they immediately abandoned their evil scheme, which could inspire nothing but the condemnation and contempt of the French people.

A reporter calling in directly from Place Beauvau added news concerning the sealing off of the capital and the imminent dispatch of an envoy by the U.S. government. Treuffais smoked cigarette after cigarette. He tried other stations, all broadcasting classical or popular music, before going back to France Inter, where Gato Barbieri was playing, to be followed by an interview with an explorer about a book he had just written. At midnight the ministerial communiqué was re-aired along with some details about the comings and goings of various officials, but there was nothing concerning the actual commando group itself. On Europe 1 and RTL likewise, the same filler. After listening to the news, Treuffais told himself that all this was no reason to change his habits. He tuned in to the shortwave, found Voice of America, and right away heard the beautiful warm tones of Willis Conover. The jazz hour was to be devoted to Don Cherry. Treuffais decided to sit back comfortably, open a beer and enjoy the music.

In the farmhouse near Couzy, Buenaventura was listening to the same music with a more distracted ear. Poindexter had been forced to take two Nembutal pills and sixty drops of Nozinan. The man was knocked out. He had been laid down in an upstairs room with two beds. Meyer was on guard alongside him with a piece. Buenaventura was down in the common area with D'Arcy, who was demolishing the bottle of Scotch. Both men were eating big cheese sandwiches.

Épaulard and Cash had set off in the girl's Dauphine and were driving towards Paris on Route Nationale 14. They saw a checkpoint with spike strips and all the paraphernalia on the road out of Lagny, but only vehicles coming out of Paris were being stopped. They drove on and came to another barrier at Porte de Vincennes, this one more substantial: a gray police bus and half a dozen cops who were freezing their asses off, for it was getting colder and colder, there was a biting wind, snow was swirling, and traffic was at a crawl.

"We were lucky earlier," said Épaulard, "to get back when we did."

Cash was driving and made no reply.

"Aren't you afraid, now that the deed is done?"

"I couldn't give a shit."

"You're a wild thing," said Épaulard, trying for levity.

"If that's all you can say, you might as well keep quiet."

The Dauphine crossed half of an ever more snow-covered Paris, went up Boulevard Sébastopol, then turned right and right again so as to come back down Rue Saint-Martin. The whores were as plentiful as the cops were rare. It is well known that the riffraff are a bastion of the social order, and it was certainly not in such a neighborhood as this that the cops would be prowling tonight. Which is why the Dauphine stopped there. Épaulard and Cash got out and explored the streets. Near three different tobacco shops they found mailboxes, into each of which they slipped a few envelopes addressed variously to the chief Paris dailies, to French and foreign press agencies, and to the minister of the interior. Each envelope contained a manifesto written by Treuffais, Buenaventura, and Meyer and laboriously reproduced with felt-tip pens and lettering stencils on stolen onionskin paper.

Somewhere between two mailboxes, in one of the portes-cochères where the streetwalkers huddled shivering, draped in synthetic furs but obliged to display deep cleavage despite the cold, Épaulard had spied and contemplated an extremely beautiful whore, tall, imperious, and gaunt. The fifty-year-old, already stirred by his proximity to Cash, very nearly suggested to his companion that the two of them pay a visit to a short-time hotel; in his mind the beautiful whore and Cash were one and the same, and he envisioned possessing them simultaneously. But the thought was ephemeral, and the last of the letters were soon mailed. Cash turned to him.

"What's with you? Why the goo-goo eyes?"

"I'm freezing," babbled Épaulard, grabbing Cash and pulling her to him. She did not resist, acting intrigued but not displeased. He released her, catching his breath.

"I'm an old fool," he said with a chuckle.

"Coquettishness will get you nowhere," said Cash. "Let's get back to the car."

She took his arm and snuggled close in a casual way. They got back in the Dauphine, left Paris, and were halted three times at police roadblocks. Each time they were made to open the trunk, and the uniforms played the beams of their flashlights over the interior of the car. They were not detained. The anxiety occasioned by these stops heightened Épaulard's emotional state. He fell prey to a wild joy. With Épaulard at the wheel now and Cash cuddled up against him, the poorly heated Dauphine bounded through the snow until it reached Couzy at three thirty in the morning. It was Saturday.

# 14

DURING the Friday-to-Saturday night, the minister of the interior got very little sleep. He conferred with representatives of the police, the gendarmerie, the army, and RG, issued a communiqué, had himself informed of the precise circumstances of the kidnapping, and placed Madame Gabrielle and her personnel in police custody along with two johns present in the brothel at the time of the action and a few other call girls from her stable. He personally entrusted the conduct of the investigation to a certain Commissioner Goémond, who was temporarily without any particular assignment but had always proved himself exceptionally devoted to the State. He updated the Élysée, Matignon, Foreign Affairs, and the United States. He ordered a vast raid on leftist circles. He prepared to seek authorization from the State Security Court, albeit after the fact, for such nighttime searches.

At five fifty on Saturday morning he went up to the top floor of the ministry for a nap. At seven fifteen he was woken by his chief of staff, who had not slept at all and was haggard and unshaven.

"Something rather astonishing has occurred," announced the chief of staff.

"Do tell."

"Apparently the kidnapping was filmed."

"Filmed? What do you mean? By the leftists?"

"No, no. There are two guys from RG downstairs. It would seem that a freelancer working for the SDECE was staked out across the street from Club Zero with a movie camera. Hmm. The purpose being to create dossiers. Hmm. To develop means, you see, of exerting pressure on the notables who patronize this establishment. And, well, it appears that this guy, this freelancer for the SDECE, filmed the operation; the SDECE has not informed us officially of this, and there's the rub, because our information apparently originates from infiltrated RG elements."

"Infiltrated? How so, infiltrated?" demanded the minister, still half-asleep. "What is this horseshit?"

"I brought you coffee. Here, if you wish."

"Yes please. No, no sugar. I repeat, what is this horseshit?"

"An RG guy," explained the chief of staff, "or a guy in their pay, infiltrated into the SDECE's Grabeliau faction, was, uh, the one who gave them this information."

"What information? Gave who? What are you telling me, for Christ's sake?"

"The information," said the chief of staff patiently, "that the Grabeliau faction of the SDECE had a guy staked out across from the club, a guy with a camera, who was supposed to film important clients with a view to creating dossiers on them ... This information was conveyed to the RG by an operative whom they had infiltrated into the SDECE."

The minister finished his cup of coffee and dabbed his chin with a paper napkin. His gaze was unwavering and hard. His jowls trembled.

"Where is this guy, this cameraman?"

"That is the question," the chief of staff answered elegantly in English.

The minister leapt from his bed and nodded soberly. Barefoot, in blue pajamas, he went into the bathroom and plugged in his electric razor. The chief of staff dogged his footsteps, rubbing his lip with his forefinger.

"This story stinks," said the minister.

"It stinks even more," agreed the chief of staff, "when you think that the two RG guys downstairs say that it will be necessary to negotiate with the Grabeliau faction to get hold of the film."

"Send the two guys to Goémond," said the minister. "For Christ's sake! It should be obvious that there's no way we're ever going to deal with the Grabeliau faction. Not the ministry in any case. Send a detailed memo to Goémond, so that he clearly understands the situation, and send him the two jokers."

"Very well," said the chief of staff, but he did not budge.

"What else do you want?"

"Goémond is not authorized to negotiate."

"For Christ's sake!" said the minister again. "To negotiate what?"

"The films. The Grabeliau faction will demand the removal of the sanctions, the rehiring of fired officials, and, uh, this is about the SAC and, as you well know, those expelled from the SAC have made common cause with the Grabeliau faction.* So the faction will certainly want financial support restored to the dissidents and a halt to legal action against the Vexin World Druidic Brotherhood..."

---

*Service d'Action Civique, an unofficial parallel police force (1960–1981) reporting directly to de Gaulle and his successors.

The minister pursed his lips and shaved for a moment or two without speaking. Then:

"The statesman's job is no cakewalk!" he said with vehemence.

He put the razor down and returned to the bedroom, the chief of staff still trotting at his heels.

"I can't accept this," added the minister, sitting down on the edge of the bed and looking for his cigarettes.

"Here, have one of mine," said the chief of staff, proffering a pack of Gauloises. "Hold on, I have a light. Here. There we are. Hmm. There is another solution. Suppose we have Goémond shut them down, try to settle their hash by intimidation. And while we're at it nab as many operatives of the Grabeliau faction as possible, including SAC dissidents. We could even accuse them of being in cahoots with the kidnappers, so discrediting everybody in one fell swoop. As for the films, we're bound to get them by applying a little third degree to these gents. Some of them will surely squeal."

"That means breaking some crockery."

"The abscess has to be lanced."

"Listen," said the minister. "You act for the best. I reserve the right to intervene personally later."

"And hang me out to dry?"

"Well, you know how it is. Eventually, yes."

"Very well," said the chief of staff, displaying no chagrin. "I'll phone Goémond."

"That's right," said the minister. "In the meantime, I'll do some thinking."

# 15

# CRUDE PROVOCATION AGAINST PROGRESS OF THE POPULAR UNION

Two policemen and the chauffeur of the Ambassador of the United States shot by an armed group of "leftists." Ambassador abducted.

---

## THE WORKING-CLASS AND DEMOCRATIC FORCES READYING A VIGOROUS RESPONSE TO THE PROVOCATEURS

# 16

ÉPAULARD awoke with a start and sat up in bed in a single motion. It took him a few seconds to recognize the bedroom. A brilliant light shone through the gaps in the shutters and shimmered through the irregular windowpanes. Meyer was lying on his side in the next bed. His mouth open, he was snoring slightly. As Épaulard was looking at him, he groaned and turned over to face the wall, using both hands to pull the bedclothes up over himself. It was not very warm in the bedroom. Épaulard's breath formed white plumes.

The fifty-year-old looked at his watch. Ten o'clock—ten in the morning, to judge by the broad daylight outside. The man got out of bed quietly; he saw no reason to wake Meyer up. He had slept in his underclothes and sweater. He took his pants from the back of a chair next to the bed and slipped into them. He was pensive. The details of the night before came back to him. He reviewed everything in his head. One dead and two seriously wounded, so the radio had said. Nothing to boast about.

Épaulard took his automatic from under the pillow, put it in his jacket pocket and silently left the room. In the hallway, he went and opened the next door along. Buenaventura was sitting on a chair reading a crime novel. Alongside him another chair held a full ashtray, a pack of Gauloises, a book of matches, an automatic and a spare magazine. Ambassador Poindexter was lying in his bed, his upper body slightly elevated on the pillows, eyes closed, glasses askew, and lower lip flapping.

"Hello," said Épaulard. "Hasn't he woken up yet?"

"He's been half-awake for hours. He keeps going back to sleep. He's not agitated. I have no problem with him."

The ambassador opened his eyes. His hands fumbled with his glasses as he tried but failed to straighten them.

"You're m-mad!" he cried in a furry voice. "You people are m-mad."

"See?" said the Catalan. "He's coming to. He doesn't keep saying 'Have a heart.'"

"I want to speak to your leader," announced Poindexter. "I insist—"

He was burbling. His eyes closed once more.

"Mad!" he repeated, his voice clearer now, and then he fell asleep again.

"You okay? Holding up?" Épaulard asked Buenaventura.

"Yeah."

"No regrets?"

"No regrets. What about you?"

"Me neither," stated Épaulard.

"You can get out now," said the Catalan. "Go back to Paris. The main part is over. No point you running risks for something you don't believe in."

"Forget it," replied Épaulard. "Look, I'm going down to have a bite and a drink, then I'll be back up to relieve you."

"There's no hurry. I don't feel tired."

"Okay."

Épaulard reclosed the door and started down to the ground floor. In the common area a fine big fire flamed in the hearth.

Cash was sitting next to it in an upholstered armchair with a bowl of café au lait on her knees into which she was dunking a piece of buttered baguette. She was wearing a red flannel dressing gown over black pajamas and on her feet were white mules.

"You are delightful," said Épaulard with sincerity.

"You're not going to go on using *vous* with me, are you?"

The fifty-year-old shrugged and descended the last few stairs. Cash got up and set her bowl and bread down on the table.

"Come and sit by the fire," she said. "I'll bring you some coffee and bread and butter."

Épaulard nodded, filled with gratitude. While Cash was in the kitchen he went over to the windows, whose shutters were open, and the feeling of comfort and joy that he had been experiencing for the last few moments only grew as he contemplated the snow blanketing the countryside. The flakes had been coming down all night long. At present a white sun shone over a deep silky layer, unctuous as lard, as crème Chantilly, or as champagne ice cream.

Then Épaulard turned around, and the feeling of comfort vanished when he noticed a Sten gun lying on the bench beside the table.

"What is that thing?" he cried.

"It's a submachine gun," Cash replied from the kitchen.

"I see that. Where did it come from?"

"It's mine. A family heirloom."

"Well, bravo. But what the hell is it doing here?"

"It could be useful, don't you think?"

"Sweetie," said Épaulard, "get it through your head that if the cops find us, we give up. Even at my age I prefer the can to a coffin. Kindly do me the favor of disassembling that thing and putting it away, wherever you like, but I don't want to see it."

He went into the kitchen, where Cash was buttering bread.

"Yes, boss," said the girl.

Épaulard ruffled her hair.

"I mean it," he said, smiling.

"I know, boss."

On the kitchen table a Melody Boy tuned to France Inter Paris 514 was playing Nat King Cole, "Route 66."

"Did you catch the ten o'clock news?" asked the ex–shark fisherman, ex–FTP Resistance fighter, ex-killer, and ex-loser, as he played with Cash's hair. "What did they say?"

"Nothing of interest. A thousand leftists questioned in Paris."

"Shit!"

"What? That was predictable, wasn't it?"

"Yes. Shit just the same."

"The papers got our text but refer to it only indirectly, as if they don't know yet what they are going to do."

"It's true they don't know."

"We stopped the minister of the interior from sleeping: he spent the night at Place Beauvau conferring and taking measures. There was another announcement along the lines of 'Republican order will be maintained.' In Marseilles, they arrested some neo-Poujadist shopkeepers with dynamite in their car."

"And the Ford Consul?"

"No mention."

"Probably means they've found it," said Épaulard.

Cash put the bread on a gaily decorated tin tray, added a bowl, and poured milk and coffee.

"How many sugars?"

"Two. What else did they say?"

"A few idiotic reactions," replied Cash, sugaring the café au lait, picking up the tray and the radio and going back into the common area with Épaulard right behind her. "The CP condemns what it calls provocation, naturally. The PSU considers that the revolutionary front is put at risk by this irresponsible act.* The Communist League calls for mass violence as opposed to adventurist *coups de main*. The Libération news agency has distributed a communiqué from a so-called New Red Army denouncing petty-bourgeois nihilists—that's us—who are objectively complicit with the power structure and proposing the slogan 'Down with All Little Neumanns!' "

"Neumann? You mean like Alfred E. Neuman?" asked Épaulard in alarm.

"Heinz Neumann," Cash clarified, placing the tray and radio on the table. "A guy who had something to do with the Canton Commune in December 1927."

"I see," said Épaulard. He sat down with a bowl in front of him. His brow was furrowed. He kept casting brief glances at Cash. The girl had sat down opposite him with her elbows on the table, contemplating the fifty-year-old, half smiling, and resting her chin on her bumping fists.

"You are a weird girl," said Épaulard.

"And you're a stupid old fool," retorted Cash. "I waited for you for an hour last night in my room. Why didn't you come?"

Épaulard choked on his bread and butter, playing for time.

"As a matter of fact," he said, "the idea occurred to me."

*Parti Socialiste Unifié.

"I should hope so!" cried Cash.

"But," Épaulard went on, "I hesitated . . . I mean, I wondered. And . . . while I was wondering . . . well, shit! . . . I fell asleep."

He looked at Cash, who was trying not to burst out laughing.

"I'm sorry," he added.

"Some man!" the girl exclaimed. "He goes to sleep wondering, and he's sorry. What a joke! Hey, you want to make love to me or not?"

"Yes."

"Okay. Tonight then. Finish your coffee. Come for a walk."

"Okay," said Épaulard.

He drank and got up. "I'm going to have to go up and relieve Buenaventura," he noted.

"What a stupid old fool!" said Cash. "I'm in for a pathetic romance, I can just feel it."

She went outside into the sunshine. Épaulard followed her. He felt shitty. Cash waited for him and took his arm. They circled the farm with the girl's head on the old fool's shoulder. Through the open door of the former stables they saw D'Arcy asleep, buried up to the neck in rotting straw. The alcoholic was pulling faces in his slumber.

A little while later, the couple went back into the farmhouse. Épaulard felt lighthearted now.

"Tonight," Cash repeated, and the man went up to spell Buenaventura.

# 17

At eleven o'clock on Saturday morning, the minister of the interior's chief of staff received Goémond.

"How far have you got?"

The commissioner clasped his hands beneath his chin with forefingers raised on either side of his mouth, which made his expression even sourer than usual. He was a fairly tall man, but he stooped so badly that he managed to seem stunted. His body swam in a large black shapeless overcoat. His pear-shaped head was endowed with an intellectual's wide waxen brow, depleted eyebrows, and a receding chin. A sketchy mustache did not improve things.

"Come on, Goémond, let's have it."

"We've found the Ford Consul used in the abduction. In a Champs-Élysées underground parking garage, as I told you over the phone. No usable fingerprints. Fiber fragments, dust, all that has gone to the lab. We've still not discovered anything that would allow for quick action."

"Unfortunate, very unfortunate," said the chief of staff in an angry tone. "I suppose you know that we have only until noon Monday, according to their sort-of manifesto?"

Goémond produced a Dutch cigarillo and lit it morosely.

"Well, carry on," said the chief of staff. "Hurry it up."

"The car," said the commissioner, "belongs to a computer

specialist. No hope there: it was stolen. In the parking garage nobody saw anything, noticed anything. What a world!"

Goémond gave a deep sigh. The chief of staff drummed his fingers on his desk.

"Let me come now," he said, "to the matter of the woman, Gabrielle. She is still in custody, and griping. Still, maybe she'll help with Identi-kit pictures of the two guys who..."

"The facts!" cut in the chief of staff, exasperated. "Get to the facts, Goémond, the facts!"

"Excuse me?"

"I couldn't care less about your normal procedures. For the love of God, tell me what's happening with the two maverick RG guys!"

"Maverick is right," replied Goémond. "For a start they are not even RGs. They claimed they were 'correspondents.' I very quickly let them know that this was no time for joking. Locked them up for two hours. They weren't expecting that. They really believed they could get us to let Grabeliau and his group off the hook for their separatist tendencies and abandon our prosecution of the Druidic Brotherhood. Mind you, these are just details. I let them know that French justice cannot be so easily manipulated."

"Stop your tomfoolery, Goémond," said the chief of staff in a threatening tone. "What do I care about how you do your job? Do you have the confounded film? That's all I want to know."

"I have the identity of the man who did the filming, one Jean-Pierre or Jean-Paul Bouboune. We are looking for him. We'll catch him, never fear."

"When?"

Goémond spread his arms wide.

"Obviously," he said, "we'd catch him more quickly if only

we made concessions to the Grabeliau group but, as I say, I told those gentlemen that that was impossible."

The chief of staff gazed at his policeman with loathing.

"That's all you have to tell me?"

"That's all."

"Very well. Get back to work, Goémond. We have both lost too much time already."

Goémond rose. He still wore the same lugubrious expression.

"You'll phone me?"

"What about?"

"If there is any news."

"You will be informed. Good day, Goémond."

# 18

A FEW YEARS earlier, in the run-up to the presidential elections, the SAC had undergone a series of purges, including that of Joseph Grabeliau, the agency's national secretary. By no means prepared to die poor and powerless, Grabeliau took his archives with him and undertook to set up his own networks within various security and police organizations, networks that he financed in several ways. At the same time, he became the grand master of the World Druidic Brotherhood of Vexin. He was arrested some months later along with several of his top advisers and charged with extortion. When the U.S. Ambassador was abducted, Joseph Grabeliau was incarcerated in Fresnes Prison. At noon the next day he was released provisionally on medical grounds. That same evening he would go to bed in Madrid. A few hours after Grabeliau's plane took off, two police officers picked up the felon Bouboune in a full-board lodging house in Enghien. In his room they found the Sankyo movie camera and a dozen or so reels of 8-mm film. They delivered everything, man and camera and film, to Commissioner Goémond.

# 19

TREUFFAIS had bought several morning newspapers, and at around four thirty in the afternoon he went down again and bought *Le Monde* and *France-Soir*, along with a can of mediocre choucroute. He went back upstairs to his apartment. After closing the door he saw his reflection in the hallway mirror and sighed. A four-day beard, red eyes, pimples, wild hair, shirt filthy and rumpled under a jacket showing four or five new cigarette burns. He put the choucroute away in a kitchen cabinet, fetched the old Radialva from the bedroom and installed himself in the bathroom with the radio and the newspapers. He ran the water for a bath and flipped thorough the papers. Hardly any fresh news. Treuffais had already learned from the radio that statements had reached newspapers and press agencies, mailed overnight from Paris and signed by the Nada group, taking credit for the kidnapping of the ambassador and demanding the nationwide publication of a manifesto and the payment of a two-hundred-thousand-dollar ransom by the State. The authorities had been given forty-eight hours to respond; the deadline was Monday at noon. In the event of a refusal, the ambassador would be executed. If the State agreed to the terms, the manifesto must be published immediately in the press and broadcast over radio and television. And new instructions would then be sent by the Nada group concerning the payment of the ransom.

*Le Monde* had already summarized and analyzed the manifesto. "The style is disgusting," the paper said, "and the childishness of certain statements of an archaic and unalloyed anarchism might raise a smile in other circumstances. In the present situation, however, they inspire disquiet, a deep anxiety in face of the nihilism embraced, seemingly with delight, by this Nada group, which chose such an apt name for itself but which, in its text as in its actions, expresses itself in an utterly unjustifiable way."

The bathtub was full. Treuffais turned off the faucets, undressed and got into the water. There he went on with his reading, letting the dirt wash off his body slowly. According to the editorialist of *France-Soir*, the terrorists of the Nada group were aping the Tupamaros in demanding the publication of their manifesto. But it needed to be stressed that following the example of the Tupamaros made no sense, especially in France, which was a democratic and certainly not an underdeveloped country. If sometimes violent protest had, alas, become part of French life, political terrorism met neither the needs nor the desires of the population. The Nada group was surely beginning to realize this already, and the editorialist hoped that reason would carry the day.

Meanwhile *Le Monde* also gave lengthy coverage to the police operations and asked who profited from the infernal cycle of violence and repression. Under the title "A Dark Page," a jurist with a reputation for seriousness drew an imbecilic parallel between the blackness of the misdeed and the blackness of the anarchist flag. A whole page was devoted to communiqués and declarations from various organizations and personalities, with a special sidebar for the points of

view of fifteen leftist groups. Treuffais almost fell asleep in
his bath and the newspapers fell into the water. He cursed
and set them to dry on the edge of the tub. He washed his
hair furiously, scratching his scalp with his fingernails. Mentally, he replayed the bitter exchange he had had with Buenaventura on the previous Monday in the Catalan's filthy
room, with playing cards strewn on the floor, cigarette butts
in a bowl, and Buenaventura standing in shadow with his
back to the window lit up by the street signs outside.

"You're not really saying that we should abandon the
operation?"

"Yes, I am," said Treuffais.

"So drop out if you want."

"You don't understand. I don't want to split from you.
I'm just asking you to suspend the operation until we've had
time to discuss it."

"No dialogue is possible between us now. I'm sorry, Treuffais, but you've gone over to the other side."

"Damn it, Buen, it's because I'm a libertarian communist
that I'm asking you to postpone the operation until we have
had time to think things over."

"Libertarian communist my ass. You all catch the bug—
you're not the first case I've seen; you all catch it, the political bug, the compromise bug, the Marxist bug. Get the fuck
out, Treuffais. I already know exactly what you want to say
to me, and the official press will be saying the same thing in
five days. Stop so we can talk? You must be kidding. We
know what a lot of good that does. Let me remind you that
my father died in Barcelona in '37."

"Yes, and I've had it up to here with hearing you say it.
It's not because your father got himself killed during an
insurrection that his surviving son is smarter than the next

guy. In fact you're probably stupider. You're falling under the spell of terrorism, and that's really stupid. Terrorism is only justified when revolutionaries have no other means of expressing themselves and when the masses support them."

"Is that all you have to say?"

"Yes," said Treuffais, suddenly exhausted and sick with despair.

"I'll convey your remarks to my comrades. And now, get the fuck out."

"Buen, we've known each other for four years and—"

"Get the fuck out before I knock your teeth out."

"I'm going. I don't want it to come to that, it would be too vile. This is truly vile."

Treuffais rinsed himself off, got out of the bathtub, and went to shave at the sink. What stank was not the fact of disagreeing with someone with twisted ideas; it was the fact of having loved him and thought for four years that they were fighting shoulder to shoulder.

# 20

"HAVE a seat, Madame Gabrielle. This won't take much longer, then you'll be able to return home. But I must ask you to take a look at these photos."

The brothel keeper nodded with a sigh. She was getting used to this. Goémond walked around so as to be next to her and leant a hip against her side of his desk. He was holding two folders, one of which contained enlargements of stills from the film shot by the felon Bouboune. The commissioner showed the brothel keeper the pictures one at a time.

"Oh! Why, yes!" exclaimed Madame Gabrielle. "Yes, yes. Where did they come from, these photos?"

"The police are well organized," answered Goémond unwisely.

"If they were, none of this would have happened!" retorted the madam. "I pay a stiff enough price. And I have been given enough assurances to have every right to expect . . ."

"Do you recognize these men?" Goémond cut in.

Madame Gabrielle's lips continued to move silently for a moment, then she gave another sigh and got to work.

"It's not very clear," she said, "but yes, this older guy. And then this one with all that hair. They're the ones who came in and attacked us. I didn't see the others—they put those drapes over my head. I thought I was going to suffocate. I have at least two thousand francs' worth of damage," she went on irately, "but that's nothing! Think of my business losses, commissioner. Do you realize that my operation is screwed? Screwed!"

"We'll see about that. Let's get back to the photos."

"I told you, I didn't see the others. Just those two bastards!"

The commissioner pointed out a third, rather heavyset individual.

"And this one? Your, ahem, escort, who was with the ambassador, also recognized the older guy, but she said it was this one who came into the bedroom with him. She didn't see the long-haired one."

"Quite possible. I didn't see what went on after they put those drapes over my head. There *were* more of them. But I didn't see them."

"Okay," said Goémond, closing the folder. "Now look at these."

He handed the madam a thicker sheaf of photographs. He held out very little hope. Goémond had assembled every picture he could find of leftist demonstrators with slingshots. The images varied greatly in quality, shots taken during various demonstrations and riots since 1968. Unfortunately, it now seemed almost certain that Madame Gabrielle never saw the slingshot user who murdered the motorcycle cop. Goémond was relying far more on the guys at Anthropometry, at present comparing images taken from the film, photos of leftists on file, and a set of pictures of unidentified individuals wearing bandanas as masks—more slingshot artists. The commissioner was therefore taken aback when the madam let out a vengeful cry.

"There he is!" she exclaimed, pointing. "There he is, the long-haired creep. He is much clearer here. I can see his evil eyes! He has a look, you can't imagine. The way he looked at me!"

"Well, this is a beauty!" muttered Goémond, following the direction of Madame Gabrielle's finger, which was placed on an angry face.

It was purely by chance that the face in question figured there at all. The picture had in fact been clipped to highlight a sling shooter with a motorcycle helmet, ski goggles, and a handkerchief over his mouth. He was caught in full motion, using his teeth as he tried to prevent the handkerchief, which masked him and protected him in some measure from tear gas, from slipping down. But he was not the one that the madam had recognized: instead, it was the long-haired guy, whose ferocious visage could be seen just over the shoulder of the masked sling shooter.

"Looks like you're right," said Goémond as he compared the picture of the demonstrator with the fuzzy still from the film that showed the longhair opening the Ford Consul's right-hand door. "Are you sure though?" he asked mechanically.

"Well, listen, I couldn't swear to it, but..."

"Don't worry, you'll never be asked to."

"Anyway, I think it's him."

"I'm going to get further details. Have a glance at the other photos anyway. You never know, you might score a twofer. It happens."

Offended by his vulgarity, Madame Gabrielle shot a glacial glance at the commissioner. He paid no attention, went and half opened the door to his office and spoke in low tones to someone outside in the hallway. Then he closed the door again and came back to the madam. She had almost finished going through the photos, but her heart was no longer in it.

"So, may I go now?" she asked.

"Just a few more minutes. The guys at Anthropometry are trying to identify the individual."

"But that will take hours!"

"No, no, no," said Goémond gently. "They have a computer. Just a matter of minutes."

And indeed, twenty-five minutes later, a new set of photographs was brought to Madame Gabrielle, much clearer this time, just twelve of them, and she had no trouble identifying her hirsute assailant.

"Buenaventura Diaz," Goémond kept saying as he leant against the doorjamb and smiled at a police officer. "Why do we put up with scum like this within our national borders? Oh well. I know this Longuevache Hotel—it's a gambling den full of Americans. Let's go."

"Do I get to go home now, yes or no?" protested Madame Gabrielle from the middle of the room.

"Yes you do, but remain available. Duty officer, take Madame home."

## 21

"I'M PERFECTLY awake now," declared Richard Poindexter. "I want to speak to your leader."

"There is no leader," said Épaulard.

"All right, but you know what I mean."

"We don't have a leader. You can talk to me if you want
to talk to someone."

The ambassador passed a coated tongue over his plump
little lips.

"Would you have a cigarette?"

Épaulard tossed him the pack of Gauloises and the book
of matches lying on the chair next to him.

"Don't try to start a fire or throw anything in my face."

"What? Oh, no, I'm not a fool."

Poindexter lit a Gauloise.

"May I know what time it is?"

"A quarter to six in the evening. It's Saturday."

"I see. I was drugged."

"A soporific," said Épaulard. "Nothing dangerous, but it
might upset your stomach."

"Right now, on the contrary, how to put it, I could eat a
horse."

"We'll have something brought up for you. Give me back
the matches instead of trying stupidly to hide them in your
bed. You say you're not a fool, but it's hard to believe it when

I see that. You should realize that your life is hanging by a thread."

The ambassador took the matchbook from under his bedclothes and tossed it to Épaulard with a wry pout.

"Good," said Épaulard. "I'll let them know to bring you up something to eat."

He stood up and stamped on the floor with his heel. He kept his automatic in his hand in case the diplomat got any more smart ideas. Then he sat back down.

"For a prisoner everything serves, everything has a purpose," Poindexter said dreamily. "As a rule he doesn't yet know himself what that purpose is. I was a prisoner in Germany. You too, perhaps?"

"Don't try to make me talk about myself."

The ambassador chuckled. The door opened. D'Arcy came in.

"What's up?"

"He's wide-awake. He's hungry."

"You want a sandwich?" the alcoholic asked the ambassador. "Because you could also have something hot, but then you'd have to wait till dinnertime, quite a while."

"As you wish, my friend," said Poindexter. "I see I'm in good hands. I feel like a clam at high tide."

"It's obvious you're a diplomat, smartass," remarked D'Arcy. "I'll bring you a sandwich." To Épaulard, he added: "And relieve you."

"Just what exactly are you?" Poindexter asked when the alcoholic had left. "Maoists?"

"You'll find out later, er, smartass," said Épaulard with annoyance.

What exactly was he? He couldn't fucking say, and it bugged him.

"May I get dressed?" asked Poindexter.

"No."

"Are you expecting to hold me for long?"

"You'll see."

"Or to kill me?"

"If I told you that, where would be the surprise?" said Épaulard.

"I have no ashtray," Poindexter complained.

"Throw your ash on the floor."

The ambassador went quiet, smoking and looking at Épaulard, who was looking at him. After a moment he spoke again.

"Political kidnapping is not appropriate for a civilized people."

"I'm not a civilized people."

"Very funny," said Poindexter with a disdainful smile.

Épaulard made no reply.

"Aren't you going to try and convince me of the correctness of your political views?" asked the ambassador, staring at his cigarette.

"No."

"I thought that was customary in such circumstances."

"Kiddo, you were a high-level servant of the State. Now you are nothing, just a thing."

"Why not just say it: a piece of shit."

"No, a thing. A pitiful thing."

"You're anarchists," said Poindexter. "I can tell because you said 'servant of the State' with such hatred."

D'Arcy came in with two sandwiches on a plate.

"All right," said Épaulard. "I think this conversation ends right here."

He rose. He covered D'Arcy with his automatic as the

alcoholic placed the two sandwiches on the ambassador's knees and stepped back with the plate.

"Don't trust him," said Épaulard. "The guy is a talker. He comes off as straightforward, but he's slimy. He's fishing for information."

"Got it."

D'Arcy took the automatic and sat on the chair.

"Later," said Épaulard, and left.

"It's devilishly cold in this house, don't you think?" said Poindexter to D'Arcy.

"Shut up, you!" replied the alcoholic. "Be quiet or I'll flatten you with this gun. I don't feel like chatting."

"As you wish," said Poindexter, huddling up and pulling the covers over him. The two of them stayed still, watching each other like a pair of china dogs, as the ambassador chewed his sandwiches.

# 22

COMMISSIONER Goémond's expression grew more and more mournful, although with him this did not signal sadness. He contemplated the room of Buenaventura Diaz. He circled it cautiously, leaning over to make out the titles of two or three books piled up by the bed. His deputies circled in the opposite direction, sniffing about.

"Look here," said one of them, "an anarchist pamphlet, *Black and Red*—plain enough, I'd say."

"You're a fool, man," said Goémond. "That's a novel by Stendhal."

"Excuse me if I beg to differ," said the deputy, "but this, this talks about 'anarchist collectives in revolutionary Spain.' You must be mixed up."

"Let's see. Oh, it's true. That's strange, I would have sworn ... but you're right: I must have been thinking of *The Charterhouse of Parma*. Okay, go through everything. I'm going back downstairs."

On the ground floor Goémond found the manager, whose name was Édouard, and showed him a photo of Buenaventura.

"Yes, yes, that's him all right," said the man, pale and sweating.

"People play cards at your place?"

"Huh?"

"Poker games at night at your place? Who comes here to play poker at night? Eh?"

"I don't know."

"Okay, I'll tell you. Americans. Poker is a game played by crooks and Americans. But there are no crooks in your establishment, right?"

"I can swear to that, commissioner."

"Americans then. American deserters I wouldn't wonder."

"I know nothing about that myself, I swear."

"Stop swearing," said Goémond.

At this juncture a new deputy came into the manager's office.

"I'm coming from the station," he said. "I have the photographs. Friends of the dago that we have files on."

"Sit down," said Goémond to Édouard. "You're going look at these for me."

"Whatever you want, I sw—I assure you, commissioner. I can't say I know everyone that comes and goes, but I'll try."

"You do that. You try."

The photos were placed on the table in two piles. In one pile, American deserters; in the other, French friends of Buenaventura Diaz. Édouard the manager scrutinized them as intently as he could. Among the deserters, he said he fancied he recognized a few. Among the French, he put his finger on one particular snapshot.

"This one, I'm certain."

Goémond noted the image's number and consulted the file: Treuffais, Marcel Eugène, b. 3/4/41, Paris X / PSU 60–62 / Libertarian Assn of Paris XV (Errico Malatesta Group) 62–63 / Worker-Student Action Cttees, Paris XV 68. Etc.

The deputy leant over to Goémond.

"Wasn't in the film."

"I know."

Édouard the manager continued his perusal but could make no further identifications.

"This guy," said Goémond, waving the picture of Marcel Treuffais, "this guy, did he come here often?"

"Yes, yes. Two or three times a week for a period."

"What period?"

"Last year. Or I should say, in the spring."

"And before that?"

"Don't think so."

"And since?"

"Yes, yes. But less frequently."

"When was the last time you saw him?"

"Well, come to think of it, the beginning of the week, Tuesday, no, Monday evening, at least I think so. They were arguing, if that helps you at all, commissioner, sir."

"Arguing?"

"Yes, at any rate that was my impression. Diaz and he were exchanging insults. In Diaz's room, I mean. But I overheard them, I mean I had gone upstairs because the toilet was clogged. I shouldn't bore you with such details, but the fact is I was up there with my plunger and I heard them through the door tearing into each other."

"A sexual conflict?"

"No, no. More like political, you might say. I mean one of them was calling the other a Marxist. Or a revolutionary. I wasn't really paying attention."

"That's not very clear," said Goémond. "We'll get back to it."

"Why are you looking for him, this Diaz?" asked Édouard the manager.

"You mind your own business. Listen, though, he's not wanted, got it?"

"Got it, commissioner. But if he comes in, I'll phone you, huh?"

"Yes, do that."

"Will I have problems?"

"We'll see," said Goémond. "Your joint is illegal, a gambling den."

"That's not true, I swear. In any case, how am I supposed to know what goes on in the rooms? I don't listen at doors."

"I'm not after gambling anyway," said Goémond. "Fly right and you'll have no trouble. And if you see any of the guys in these photos you'd be well advised to get on the horn to me fast, you follow?"

"Yes, yes."

The telephone rang. The deputy picked up, listened, and handed the receiver to Goémond.

"Yes," said Goémond. "Are you sure? Since '62? That makes sense. Yes, I understand. I'll note it."

The deputy passed him something to note with. Goémond noted: André. Épaulard. Date of birth. Date of return to France. ("He didn't lose any time, that one," he observed.) Address. Goémond thanked his interlocutor briefly. He hung up. He drew the deputy out into the hallway.

"They have identified another one on file thanks to the film and had this confirmed by the brothel keeper. An old file. A hardened veteran of the Communist Resistance. National Liberation Front networks in the Algerian war. I have his address. You come with us."

On Rue Rouget-de-Lisle the cops double-parked, almost completely blocking the narrow street. Goémond went up with two men. A third stopped by the concierge's lodge and rejoined the others on a landing with a passkey. They went in; they gave the place a once-over; they came up with the Chinese automatic at the back of the armoire.

"Won't the minister be happy!" said one of the deputies. "We're going to treat him to an international conspiracy, and a monster one at that."

Goémond shot a withering glance at him, and he fell silent.

A man was left on guard at the apartment while the commissioner and his two most reliable officers set off for the fifteenth arrondissement. Night had completely fallen by the time they reached Treuffais's. The unemployed philosophy teacher answered at the second ring of the doorbell. He opened the door halfway.

"What is—"

Goémond kicked the door panel with all his might. Treuffais was thrown backwards. The three policemen were very quickly inside the apartment. As soon as he heard the door slam shut behind him, the commissioner grabbed Treuffais, who was regaining his balance, by the hair, banged his head against the wall, landed a left to his kidney, and kneed him in the groin. Treuffais doubled over, a croaking sound came from his throat, then he fell to his knees and vomited onto the parquet floor. Goémond recoiled just in time to avoid being splashed and sent a flying kick to the side of Treuffais's head. The young man fell to the floor and curled up against the wall. He was trying to protect himself. Goémond stamped on his hand, once again seized his hair, and dragged him along the floor through the hallway and into the living room. There he knelt down on the teacher's belly, grabbed his ears and slammed his head against the floor.

"Where is the ambassador?"

"Go fuck yourself," muttered Treuffais.

Goémond let go of him and stood up, smiling.

"Don't you want to ask me who I am? All the same, you knew right away that we were the cops, didn't you? You don't ask me what ambassador? Or what I want to talk about? You got it straightaway. Strange, huh?"

Treuffais looked at him.

"You're from the police?" the philosophy teacher exclaimed. "I don't believe you. Let me see your ID."

"Don't play dumb. It's too late for that," said Goémond, sitting down in the father's chair. "You know we're the cops. Unless of course you think we might be the CIA hunting for Poindexter. Yup, that idea must have crossed your romantic little noddle. Well, forget the romanticism and get real. We've got Buenaventura Diaz and André Épaulard. Épaulard is a hard nut. He doesn't want to talk. But your pal Diaz—I'm sure you have his measure—is a swine. Personally I find him disgusting. I've seen lots of guys roll over, but never so quickly. After a quarter of an hour he gave us your name and address. He even claimed it was you who killed the motorcycle cop. But I didn't believe him because I know that you weren't there. I am well informed, you see. No point your bothering to hold out."

Goémond smiled again and awaited a reply. None came.

"Where is Ambassador Poindexter?" the commissioner asked again.

Silence. Goémond sighed and signaled his subordinates with a nod. They grabbed hold of Treuffais and began to give him a real beating.

"When you've had enough, you can tell us," said Goémond.

# 23

MEYER, Buenaventura, Épaulard and Cash shared their meal in the common area before a superb crackling log fire. They hardly spoke. Then Buenaventura went upstairs to relieve D'Arcy with the prisoner, and the alcoholic came downstairs to eat and drink in his turn. They dawdled for hours by the fire. They shared memories. They spoke slowly.

"I don't understand your motives," said Épaulard.

"You understand your own," said Cash. "That's enough."

"If it was just up to me, this kidnapping would never have happened."

"Same here," said Meyer, who hardly ever said anything. "I was sick and tired of life as we live it, yes, and something had to give. Maybe I'd have killed my wife. Or robbed a gas station. But this...what we did? No, never. It was Buenaventura and Treuffais who cooked it all up."

"But politically it's stupid," said Épaulard.

"So you think like Treuffais then?"

"I don't know. Perhaps. I don't know what Treuffais thinks."

"Treuffais pissed his pants," said D'Arcy. "He's an intellectual. All his life he'll continue to eat shit and say thank you and cast blank ballots. But modern history doesn't give a rat's ass about shit eaters."

The alcoholic poured himself a glass.

"I drink to us," he said, his voice thick. "I drink to desperadoes. And I don't give a fuck about being politically right or stupid. Modern history created us, which only shows that civilization is on the eve of destruction one way or the other. And believe you me, I'd sooner finish in blood than in caca."

He emptied his glass.

"You're all deadly boring," he went on. "Stop talking. Can it. You're pissing me off."

Cash got up.

"I'm going to sleep. Come on, you," she said to Épaulard.

Épaulard gave a short laugh and got up too.

"Good night," he said to the others.

"Good night, comrade," said Meyer.

"Good nooky, lovebirds," said D'Arcy.

Épaulard went up. Cash had gone ahead of him and when he entered the room she was waiting for him, shivering under the covers of the double bed. Épaulard undressed with a certain nervousness, then lay down with Cash, proved to be increasingly nervous, and everything was over quickly. Épaulard seethed with shame and disappointment. After a moment or two he tried again. He thrashed about for a long time. His efforts were fruitless. Cash pushed him aside gently. With his face in the pillow, Épaulard panted like a mule and ground his teeth. Cash kissed his shoulder.

"I'm no good for anything anymore, on any level," he said.

"You old fool," said Cash tenderly. "It's the stress. The anxiety. Things will go better tomorrow."

She caressed his cheek sweetly, but Épaulard sensed her disappointment and there was nothing for it. Cash was mistaken: things would not go better tomorrow. Tomorrow they would be dead.

# 24

TREUFFAIS was semicomatose. One of the officers was kicking him without conviction. The other was casing the apartment. Seated in the father's armchair, Goémond was annoyed to see his prisoner prone on the floor and no longer responding to blows. He got up and went into the kitchen, where his subordinate was executing a summary search.

"He's still not talking?" the man asked.

Goémond shook his head.

"Did you try twisting his nuts?"

"That would be torture," said Goémond. "We do not torture in France. But, well, if he persists, we'll see. Have you found anything?"

The officer nodded and spread a few objects out on the kitchen table. A weighted blackjack. Ten or so checkbooks bearing different names. A datebook.

"Stolen checkbooks," he said.

"Slim pickings."

"I'm willing to bet they come from the BNP branch that was hit by the Gauche Prolétarienne on May 27, 1970."

"I'm not seconding your bet," said Goémond, "but you might be right. That doesn't get us very far though. Let's look at the datebook."

He flipped through it, but the pages were blank. At the back, however, was an address section. The commissioner examined this closely and found addresses for André Épaulard and Buenaventura Diaz.

"Go and call the station," Goémond told the officer. "I want guys sent immediately to check out all the addresses in this book, see if anything stinks, and whether people are home. Don't tip them off though. Use good cover stories."

"Good cover stories for visits in the middle of the night?" protested the officer.

"They'll manage it."

"Should we try addresses in the provinces too?"

"We'll try everything. But wait until tomorrow morning for the provincial ones. I'll arrange it with the ministry directly."

"Fine."

The officer went to telephone in the hallway. Goémond went back into the dingy living room. He had not had dinner; he was beginning to feel tired. Treuffais was still stretched out on the floor. The other policeman had taken off his jacket and was smoking a cigarette. A nonservice Colt .38 hung under his arm in a canvas holster.

"Still haven't decided?" Goémond asked Treuffais.

"Screw you, slimeball," mumbled Treuffais.

The officer in shirtsleeves kicked him idly.

"Don't you understand that we'll get them anyway, your pals, because we already have Diaz and Épaulard? If you helped us, you'd save a us a little time, that's all. It's not dishonorable, after all, to admit defeat when you're well and truly defeated. Myself, I call that realism. And if you help us, I could do something for you."

"You've already done too much for me, bitch."

Not bad, thought Goémond. He has decided to open his

dumb mouth. That's progress even if it's only to call me names. The commissioner nibbled at his mustache.

"You'll have your balls busted for this, I can promise you that," said Treuffais feebly. "If you really are cops, you're not done with me. Because I've done nothing, I know nothing, and you, you break in here with no warrant and torture me. I tell you, I'm going to sue you."

"Poor little lamb!" said Goémond. "It goes on about torture but doesn't even know what it's talking about."

"You can never charge me with anything because I haven't done anything," claimed Treuffais in an exhausted voice.

"Receiving stolen checks," sneered Goémond. "That'll do for starters. Then we'll consider threatening the security of the State and being an accomplice to murder. I can hold you as long as I like. And I'll hold you till you talk."

"Arrest me then. Put me in jail. You have no right to remain in my apartment and keep me here."

"No right? Rights are something I can take or leave alone."

"Okay. If that's how it is," said Treuffais, and he began to scream as loudly as he could.

Goémond bounded forward and placed the sole of his shoe on Treuffais's mouth. There was a brief struggle. The other policeman rushed over. Treuffais managed to sit up and was wailing at the top of his lungs. Goémond got a blackjack out of his jacket and hit the young man over the head. Treuffais went silent and quite limp. Somewhere on the lower floors, tenants disturbed by the racket started banging on the water pipes with broom handles.

"What do we do?" asked the officer. "Take him in?"

"I think we'll have to. Unofficial though, okay? We'll just lock him up good for now."

"With these politicals," said the policeman, "you've got to watch it. This guy might fucking well take legal action later."

"Later, son, believe me," said Goémond, "he won't be in a mood to do that."

# 25

"WHAT is it?"

"Is this Monsieur Lamour's residence?"

"Yes. This is he. What is it? Do you realize what time it is?"

"General Intelligence."

"You are from the police?"

"Yes."

"Oh, in that case, come in, come in. What can I do for you?"

Monsieur Lamour dutifully unlocked the garden gate. Two policemen followed him down a sandy path and into his detached house. Madame Lamour, in curlers, was standing worriedly by the stairs.

"What is it, Joseph?"

"These gentlemen are from the police. Go back up to bed."

"But what's going on?"

"Madame Lamour, I presume," said one of the policemen.

"Yes. What's going on?"

"Do you know a certain Marcel Treuffais?"

"That lowlife!" said Huguette Lamour.

Monsieur Lamour, director of Saint-Ange Academy, then engaged in a conversation, too short for his liking, with the two cops. Regrettably, no, he did not know Treuffais's friends. Naturally, he had nothing to do with such people, and no, the names Buenaventura Diaz and André Épaulard meant nothing to him. But what had he done now, that thug Treuf-fais?

"Just a routine verification. But one that needs to be conducted quickly and delicately. It is important that our inquiry not be widely publicized, you understand. Not before Monday morning, at any rate. I trust we may count on your discretion?"

"The French police may always count on me," declared the director of the Saint-Ange Academy.

At various other addresses throughout Paris and its sub-urbs, similar inquiries were being made on the basis of the information in Treuffais's datebook.

# 26

ANNIE Meyer was stricken with fear. This was her second night alone and she did not know where Meyer was or how many days would pass before he came home. She was drawing. Her picture showed two buildings in the desert separated from each other by a torrent of mud and shit moving at a terrifying pace. To connect the two houses, Annie drew a footbridge that seemed to her perilously frail. She rose suddenly, fancying that she heard a noise. She picked up the kitchen knife, which she was afraid of but which she kept with her wherever she went in the apartment, to defend herself against any attack. She circled the two rooms holding the knife ahead of her. Then she returned to her drawing table to put the finishing touches on her footbridge. She turned it into a hermetically closed suspended tunnel. After that she began drawing Taipings, Boxers, Thugs, Sikhs, Huns, and Mandingos rushing forward from the horizon to mount an assault on the twin houses. Then the doorbell rang.

Annie froze.

She stood rigid, holding her breath. The bell rang again, for longer this time. The young woman's teeth began to chatter. She heard or thought she heard whispering on the landing, and a shuffling of feet. At last, after several more rings, came the sound of the elevator working. Had the intruders really gone down, or was this just a trick?

After staying still for the better part of a minute, Annie tiptoed to the window that gave onto the street, opened it, and leant out. Two dark figures in overcoats had just emerged from the building, and one of them turned the pale patch of his face upward. The man pointed a finger toward the building's façade—and toward Annie.

"But there's someone up there!" she heard him say to his companion.

The young woman reared back. Her teeth clacked horribly. A moment later she heard the two men coming up by the stairs, quickly, noisily, confidently. She decided then that she was crazy, a mental case, and that Meyer had left purposely so that she would be picked up by male nurses with big dicks and taken to an asylum. As a thunder of pounding fists struck the front door, she fled to the bathroom, grabbed Meyer's straight razor and clumsily gashed her throat. The sight of the spurting blood terrified her. She screamed and rushed to the hallway just as the cops broke down the door.

"Help!" she screamed, pressing her hand to her neck in an attempt to staunch the bleeding.

# 27

AT FIRST light Cash slipped out of the bed where Épaulard was sleeping.

"Where are you going?"

"To feed my rabbits."

"Are you coming back?"

"Yes. Go back to sleep."

Cash left the room. Épaulard sat up in bed. He grimaced. His nighttime efforts had earned him aching muscles. He delved into the pockets of his pants, which were lying on the floor, and found cigarettes and matches. He smoked in the gray half-light. He could not visualize the future. He did not believe that the ransom would be paid or that he would be rich the following week. He did not even see himself living that long.

Eventually he got up and dressed. He went downstairs. In the common area the hearth was cold and dark. Buenaventura was drinking coffee and listening to the radio turned low.

"Morning," said Épaulard, coughing over his cigarette.

"Morning."

"Seen Cash?"

"She's feeding her rabbits."

"Huh," grunted Épaulard, sitting down at the table. He poured himself a cup of coffee.

"She's a strange girl," he said.

"She's a fine girl," said Buenaventura.

"Have you known her for long?"

"Fairly, yes."

"Ever sleep with her?"

"No. She didn't want me."

Épaulard looked down at his coffee.

"You've hardly slept," he remarked.

"Five hours. That's quite enough."

"Anything new on the radio?"

"Zilch. They piss me off. You can't expect them to give an answer about the ransom before the last minute. All the same, it bugs me."

Cash came in from the rear wearing a filthy reversible sheepskin jacket, blond hair in her face. She pushed the strands back with one hand.

"Everyone's up, I see . . . I'll have a cup with you."

She sat down and poured herself coffee. She turned the volume up on the radio. The transistor set began to quaver horribly.

"Shit! The batteries!"

"We don't have spares?"

"No."

"Oh shit!"

"I'll go for some at nine," said Cash. "When the stores open in Couzy."

"I'll go with you," said Buenaventura.

"Why?"

"I'm fed up with being here. It gets on my nerves."

"You go and get them with the Dauphine then. I'd as soon stay here."

"Okay."

Buenaventura stood up.

"Hey," said Cash, "you have to wait. They don't open till nine, the stores."

"Right."

The Catalan sat back down.

# 28

LEAVING his aides to attend to Marcel Treuffais, Goémond had gone home to take a nap around two in the morning. Awakened at eight by the telephone ringing, he jumped out of bed, stumbled, and picked up the phone.

"Hello?" He looked at his watch and swore inwardly on seeing the time.

"Commissioner, I believe we have them!"

On the other end of the line the voice of his subordinate quivered with the enthusiasm of youth. He gave Goémond the particulars. In the process of checking the addresses in Marcel Treuffais's datebook, they had given a hotel manager something of a grilling about a certain Véronique Cash, who was supposed to live in his establishment but who had not shown up there for two weeks.

"So what?" said Goémond irascibly.

He was exhausted. The six hours of sleep seemed to have done him no good. And he hated, he was outraged, that important developments might occur while he was sleeping. He was in a filthy temper. Standing by the bed in his burgundy pajamas, he cast a ferocious glance around his one-room kitchen-bath, a recent acquisition. He found it suddenly horrible, constricted, smelly, and grotesque.

"Seeing the girl's type, so to speak, her disreputable character, and that she seems to be more or less kept, a parasite with shameless disorderly tendencies, our guys went so far as to show him some pictures."

"Show who?"

"Well, commissioner, the manager—"

"And then what?"

"He recognized Diaz."

Goémond chewed on his mustache. With his left hand he searched for his little Dutch cigars and performed the rather gymnastic feat of lighting one without letting go of the receiver.

"This Monique—"

"Véronique, commissioner. Véronique Cash."

"This Monique or Véronique...Don't interrupt me," shouted Goémond. "This girl, is she the one with two addresses in the datebook?"

"Exactly, commissioner. Her other address is sixty-odd kilometers from Paris, out in the boondocks. So we are asking ourselves questions, and thinking of answers."

"Pascal, my boy," said Goémond, his eyes glistening, "don't you move, do absolutely nothing, while I make tracks to the Interior."

"The interior of what?" asked the subordinate, whose sleepless night had done nothing for his intelligence.

"Place Beauvau, blockhead," roared Goémond. "Await my orders!"

He hung up the phone. He took off his pajamas, skipped his morning exercise routine, dressed at top speed (white man-made-fiber shirt, chocolate-brown suit, blue tie with red stripes), and shaved electrically. Before leaving he opened the window to air out the room. Down at street level, in a well-lit snack bar ensconced on the ground floor of his building between a laundromat and a youth club, he downed a very short espresso. The building was a new one, not far from the Seine. Where stores were not established on ground floors along the street, there were white walls defaced by daubed inscriptions, often obscene, always abusive and generally threatening. Goémond paid for his coffee and left the snack bar. He got into his Renault 15, which was parked in front of a large red graffito: TREMBLE RICH PEOPLE YOUR PARIS IS SURROUNDED WE ARE GOING TO BURN IT DOWN. The car headed for Place Beauvau.

The minister of the interior's chief of staff had dark circles under his eyes.

"And that woman's suicide attempt?" he asked.

"That's just it!" exclaimed Goémond. "The Meyer woman is in the hospital—in intensive care at Hôtel-Dieu. She can't be questioned yet, but she'll make it. She has us to thank, that one, for saving her life."

"Any news on other fronts?"

"Better believe it!" said Goémond, and proceeded to put his interlocutor in the picture.

"But you have no proof," said the chief of staff. "You are just assuming that they can be found in the country at this Monique Cash's place."

Goémond corrected him automatically: "It's Véronique. And I am assuming enough to have the property surrounded."

"All right. Would you prefer CRS or mobile gendarmerie?"

"CRS."

"Well, I'd rather assign you mobile gendarmes. So as not to always have the same guys sticking their necks out. I'll call the Army Ministry for clearance. And I'll have to apprise the prefect of Seine-et-Marne, who will want to be present at the site. We'll let him know after the showdown is over, if showdown there is."

"I'd be surprised if there were a showdown," said Goémond. "French leftists have no guts. They will surrender."

"They've already killed two people, including a motor-cycle policeman."

"Nevertheless, they will surrender."

"To the contrary, I feel sure they'll start shooting," said the chief of staff.

Goémond gave him a sidelong glance and took out a little cigar, which he lit in a leisurely way to give himself time to reflect.

"Anyway," the chief of staff added, "do you think it's worth taking them alive?"

"If it were just up to me, I'd put them up against the wall, as you well know."

"I know no such thing, Goémond."

"All right, so I'm telling you now. But I'm thinking of their hostage, you see... An ambassador..."

"Indeed," said the chief of staff. "If they eliminated him during an assault, how ghastly! It so happens that a slice of public opinion entertains a thoughtless sympathy for the far left, but such sympathy would be impossible to sustain if the leftists revealed their true nature by murdering a defenseless captive in cold blood."

"Yes," mused Goémond, "and as for these people we're looking for, they have already proved their viciousness by killing two policemen."

"One policeman, Goémond. One policeman and one American house-staff member."

"You're right. What contempt for human life!" sighed the commissioner.

"It wouldn't surprise me if they murdered their hostage," said the chief of staff.

Goémond looked at him.

"And the minister, wouldn't he be surprised?"

"No."

"And the Americans, wouldn't they be surprised?"

"Goémond, a disciplined police officer should not concern himself with politics, especially international politics. Must I remind you of that?"

"No, sir. Very well, sir," said the commissioner.

# 29

TREUFFAIS was sitting on the floor against the wall with his back to it. Handcuffs chained him to a radiator. Goémond came in with his little cigar between his lips.

"Son," said the commissioner, "I came to see you before I leave. We know where your pals are, and where Ambassador Poindexter is."

Treuffais made no reply.

"Would you like a smoke?"

"Yes, I would."

Goémond took the cigarillo from his mouth and brought it close to Treuffais's.

"Assuming you don't mind your lips touching a place just touched by a cop's lips?"

"Why should I give a shit?"

Goémond shrugged, leant down and placed the cigarillo in his prisoner's mouth. Treuffais inhaled with pleasure. The commissioner straightened up.

"I like you," he said. "I'm going to be straight with you. I admit that I'm not really sure about anything. I admit I don't really know where your pals are. I admit I haven't arrested either Diaz or Épaulard."

With his left hand, Treuffais removed the cigarillo from his lips. He was shivering a little from the cold. The radiator was not on. The young man wore only a light-blue cotton shirt and very ragged corduroy pants. His body hurt and his breath was fetid, but his face was unmarked. All blows had been directed elsewhere. He contemplated Goémond thoughtfully.

"At the same time," the commissioner went on, "I think I know where they are, your buddies. If that is where they truly are, you might confirm the fact for me and save me a little time. Your pals wouldn't be any the worse for it, and as for you, it wouldn't do you any harm to show a touch of goodwill."

Silence from Treuffais.

"Apart from Diaz and Épaulard," said Goémond, "there are two other guys, and I believe they are at Véronique Cash's address in Couzy. What do you say to that?"

Treuffais had nothing to say. He merely began to shake more violently. Goémond shrugged and snatched back the cigarillo. He crushed it in his fist, rolled it into a ball, and sprinkled tobacco, embers and ash on the prisoner's head.

"Suit yourself," he said. "As for me, I'm going to Couzy. If it turns out I'm wrong, we'll resume our little chat later."

"Wait," said Treuffais. "I've had enough of this. I'll tell you where they are."

Goémond kept walking towards the door.

"They're in Corsica!" shouted Treuffais. "They took a private plane. They were going to hide out in Corsica, but I don't know exactly where. I swear that's the truth!"

"Don't bother, you poor fool," said Goémond, and left.

# 30

"HOW MAY I be of service, sir?" the man at the hardware store asked parochially.

"Six 1.5-volt batteries."

"What size, sir? We have these, and we have those."

"Those."

"Six, you said?"

"Yeah."

The storekeeper put the six batteries in a little promotional bag. Buenaventura paid and left. He did not want to return to the farmhouse right away. The inactivity was beginning to irk him. He walked past the Dauphine, parked alongside the curb, and went into a *bar-tabac* called La Civette de Couzy on the corner where the departmental road ran into the town's little main square. The Catalan stood at the bar and ordered a marc. At the end of the counter, bundled-up and dirty-faced coalmen were drinking mulled wine. A fifty-something woman with a bosom as vast as a belly was knitting behind the cash register with packets of *gris* rolling tobacco piled up behind her. Depressed by the general atmosphere of apathy, unconsciousness, booze, and humidity, Buenaventura turned his back on his marc and leant against the counter to survey the street through the glass door. The roadway was wet, but the snow had melted and only grayish, spongy, and repellent little piles of it were left in the gutter.

The Catalan would have liked Treuffais to be there. He pictured his friend playing poker with him, a game of Southern Cross with nine wild widows in a cross in the middle and a five-card deal—a rather slow variation leaving plenty of time to chat. A large gray bus full of gendarmes went by. Buenaventura reached in his pocket, produced a one-franc coin, put it on the bar, emptied his glass and quickly made his exit. A second bus passed by. The Catalan's eyes followed it as he ran for the Dauphine. The wet sidewalks were a little slippery. He got into the car. The engine was old but still warm. He wanted to leave right away and immediately wrenched the car away from the curb.

Buenaventura circled the little square and took the departmental road in the wake of the two police buses. He spotted the second disappearing around a tree-lined bend eight or nine hundred meters ahead. The Catalan accelerated. The old clunker vibrated. A rear quarter panel was completely split open by rust and rattled like scrap metal. Buenaventura reached the bend, then downshifted. Not very far ahead, a left turn off the departmental road, was the byroad, classified as "rural," which led to the farm. One of the buses had pulled up on the right shoulder of the highway while the other was parked just on the turn into the byroad and blocking the way. From both buses were pouring masses of helmeted figures shrouded in voluminous black raincoats and armed with Mousquetons. Buenaventura barely slowed as he passed. He took a worried glance at the goings-on. Units were setting off at the double down the byroad. The farmhouse, though only half a kilometer away, was invisible on account of the hilly and wooded terrain. The anarchist reckoned that the cops could get there in five to ten minutes but would probably take time to surround the farm without causing alarm—a good twenty minutes in all. Buenaventura stepped on the gas, trying to remember the topography and byways in the vicinity. He covered about two kilometers before he came to another left turn. He took it, hurrying through the melting snow. Pools of cold mud exploded beneath his tires, spattering and streaking the sides of the Dauphine and spraying the windshield. The wipers struggled. The rear of the vehicle fishtailed from one side to the other of the narrow thoroughfare.

Once he decided that he had put the farmhouse between the gendarmes and himself, the Catalan looked out for the entrance to a dirt track on his left. It appeared. He braked, but too fast. The wheels locked. The Dauphine did a double one-eighty and left the road by way of the right verge. The front wheels plunged into a ditch and the car came to a halt. Buenaventura was thrown against the wheel and the impact winded him. He opened the door and jumped out.

Beads of sweat proliferated on his skin. His jaw was clenched tight. A dull groan issued from his throat. He took off his leather coat and threw it onto the snowy ground. He went to the back of the Dauphine, leant down and took hold of the rear bumper. Bracing himself with difficulty in the mud, he pulled up on the car with all his might. His face turned red and the veins stood out on his gaunt temples. Suddenly his left foot skidded and he fell flat.

"*El Cristo en la mierda!*" he swore ferociously.

Getting to his feet, he headed to the front of the car. He pushed his way through snow-covered brambles up the opposite side of the ditch. He positioned his feet firmly against the bank, the soles of his shoes planted in the cold loam. Then he took hold of the bumper. He gave a cry. He lifted the car, the wheels left the ditch, the Dauphine rolled backwards onto the road, and Buenaventura fell onto all fours in the mud-filled trench. He suddenly felt weak. Angrily, he threw up the marc he had ingested; his nausea was controlled, salutary, and brief.

He climbed out of the ditch, retrieved his leather coat and took the wheel once more. Maneuvering carefully, he backed up to the beginning of the dirt track. Then, in first gear, he started down it with his wheels in the enormous ruts left by tractors. Gradually he picked up speed. Here and there deep puddles had formed that had to be skated over with the impetus built up. Bouncing back and forth between the sides of the ruts, the car advanced at about 40 kph in the direction of the farmhouse.

The place was still invisible to Buenaventura: copses, uneven land and the sunken track conspired to hide it from him.

The Catalan held tight to the steering wheel. His ashen countenance was contorted by anxiety and the urge to kill. The sweat had dried on his face, but he felt it soaking his torso and his clothes. He was grinding his teeth. The Dauphine debouched into open land.

The farmhouse was on a little plateau. To the west was the byroad that led up to it. To the east were the shadowy orchard, a stretch of snow-covered stubble, and Buenaventura.

Just as he reached the edge of the plateau, the Catalan noticed that, to his right and about a kilometer away, glinting dark figures with guns were snaking their way through a bosky area. The dirt track changed direction just then, leading him towards the intruders. Buenaventura stopped, got out of the Dauphine and opened the gate to a meadow. Back in the car, he drove into the field, accelerating as much as possible, so that for a moment the vehicle seemed to be flying across the clammy earth towards the farmhouse, where no sign of life was to be seen save a pale-gray wisp of smoke against the pale-gray sky.

Over to the right the glinting figures were emerging from the bosky covert, and Buenaventura saw out of the corner of his eye that they were led by a small group of men in civilian clothing wearing dark overcoats and clear-plastic capes.

All of a sudden the Dauphine pitched forward. Its wheels churned into a pile of soft greasy compost. Buenaventura went into reverse and hit the gas pedal. The clutch gave out. The engine roared to no avail as the car sank into the muck. Tucking his leather coat under his arm, the Catalan got out and began running towards the farmhouse three hundred meters away. He also began shouting at the top of his lungs.

# 31

WHEN BUENAVENTURA started shouting at the top of his lungs it was ten o'clock in the morning, and Sunday. Ambassador Richard Poindexter was eating ham and eggs brought to him in his bed. Meyer was guarding him, his pistol on the chair next to him, with half an eye on Poindexter and half on a battered science fiction novel. The others were down below. In the kitchen Épaulard and Cash were washing dishes in cold water. In the common area by the fire D'Arcy was drinking a beer and getting ready to go upstairs to sleep, having watched the ambassador from two in the morning on.

The alcoholic frowned, put his beer down and went over with heavy steps to the kitchen door.

"Hey, can't you hear anything?"

Épaulard turned.

"No," he said, but seeing D'Arcy's worried expression he frowned in his turn, reached for the faucet and turned the water off.

In the sudden silence they all heard sustained but reedy shouts. Cash, her hands still wet, opened the kitchen window, which gave onto the rear of the farmhouse. Straight away, between the dark trees, an agitated form could be seen running across the stubble, hollering and getting closer.

"It's Buen," said D'Arcy.

Épaulard's gaze raked the fields and his heart missed a beat when he spotted other figures in motion over to the left, shimmering.

"To the left," he said. "Cops."

"I'm going to check the front," said D'Arcy. "I'll get the Jaguar going. Bring the ambassador."

He left the kitchen, crossed the common area in a flash and opened the windowed front door. Beyond the land that ran from the farmhouse to the byroad, the alcoholic saw nothing to worry about. Everything was whitish and deserted. He rushed to the garage, entered, got into the car and started it up.

In the house, Cash was bounding up the stairs four at a time.

Épaulard remained at the open kitchen window watching the Catalan, who had entered the orchard. On the way Buenaventura had surrendered his coat to barbed wire. Now he was running through the dark fruit trees. He had stopped shouting for he was out of breath.

"André Épaulard! Buenaventura Diaz! Véronique Cash! All of you!" came a voice powerful and distant like the voice of Zeus. "You are surrounded!"

The megaphone transmitted a sigh. Two hundred meters away, the cops were out of breath too. Goémond paused, taking the megaphone from his mouth. Three plainclothes policemen were by his side, as well as a gendarmerie officer and his radio operator. Short-winded, the commissioner pointed silently to the operator's walkie-talkie. The radio man passed it to him. Goémond leant against the trunk of a cherry tree.

"Blue Two," he puffed. "Blue Two, can you read me? Goémond here. Over."

"Blue Two," the device responded. "We are at the western edge of the farm, on the byroad. Sixty meters from the house, along the embankment. We are not moving forward. I await your orders. An individual has just exited the farmhouse and entered the north wing. Over."

"I'll be in charge of ultimatums," said Goémond. "If fire is opened, prevent anyone from leaving in your direction. Fire on the front of the house and use grenades. Over."

"Understood. Out."

Goémond returned the walkie-talkie to the radio operator and put the megaphone to his lips once more.

"Hey! You! The guy running towards that farm! Stop immediately or we shoot. This is the police. Stop right now!"

Buenaventura began zigzagging between trees.

"Open fire on him!" ordered Goémond.

"But commissioner—" began the officer.

"Fire on him, goddammit!"

The officer glowered and turned towards his gendarmes, who were deployed to his right and twenty meters behind him.

"Estève!" he shouted. "Open fire on that guy running!"

Gendarme Estève, an elite sniper, put a knee to the ground and positioned his carbine. Buenaventura was sprinting for the farmhouse.

"Aim at his legs!" said the officer.

"Aim anywhere!" shouted Goémond.

Hesitant, Estève fired somewhat randomly. Buenaventura pivoted, flailed his arms to keep his balance but tumbled onto his back. He got up right away and threw himself headfirst against the farmhouse back door, which sprang open. The Catalan fell through, landed flat on his belly, frantically pulled his legs in beneath him and kicked the door shut with an ankle. At that moment a white cloth appeared and waved out of the kitchen window.

"They're surrendering," exclaimed the gendarmerie officer with a sigh of relief.

"It's a trick," opined Goémond.

From the farmhouse's upper floor, through a window barely wider than an arrow slit, someone opened up with a submachine gun.

# 32

CASH HAD raced up the stairs four at a time. She dashed into the ambassador's room. Meyer was on his feet with his automatic in his hand. The science fiction novel had fallen onto the floor. The brasserie waiter was visibly alarmed.

"What's happening? Who is that shouting?"

"Quick! You have to take the ambassador downstairs!" screamed Cash, rushing to the window that looked out from the front of the house.

She saw the opened garage doors. From her high vantage point she also saw a string of black-helmeted heads lined up sixty meters away along the byroad's snowy embankment.

"Shit!" she said to Meyer. "It's too late. Stay right here. Keep an eye on that fat idiot. Stay right here. I'll be back."

She disappeared instantly into the hallway and entered her room with its unmade bed. She thrust her hand under the bed and pulled out the Sten gun and magazines wrapped in rags. She fitted a magazine to the weapon. Carbine fire rang out from below. Immediately afterwards there was a ruckus at the back door of the farmhouse.

Meanwhile, standing at the kitchen window, Épaulard was paralyzed by indecision and an extraordinary torpor as he watched the Catalan spin, fall, get up and hurtle into the door. The fifty-year-old grabbed a white dish towel and waved it.

"Cease fi—"

Cash shot across the bedroom, broke the window in the hallway with the Sten's barrel and simultaneously pulled the trigger, emptying her whole magazine at random. The rounds scattered, shredding the dark branches of the dark trees.

"Fire!" cried Goémond at the top of his voice.

Electrified by his command, by the burst of submachine-gun fire, and by the fragments of wood raining down on their helmets, the gendarmes obeyed as one man. Window-panes shattered around Épaulard. Amazed that he was not hit, the fifty-year-old wheeled and made a dash for the kitchen door and got the impression that someone had given him a big clap on the back. He closed his eyes and fell flat on his stomach on the tiled floor. Above him bullets buried them-selves in the walls, ricocheted around the kitchen, shredded the sailing ship on a post office calendar, and riddled the fridge with holes.

"Where's my piece?" asked Épaulard, slurring the words, but nobody answered.

At the same time, the fire from the gendarmes was ravag-ing the hutches backing onto the farmhouse's rear, and rab-bits could be seen flying up into the air, twirling and almost exploding, and heard squealing, which added to the pande-monium.

At the same time too, the gendarmerie officer, white with fury, had taken three steps sideways and was yelling for cease-fire when half the contents of Cash's second magazine struck him in a scatter, most of the projectiles being pancaked by his bulletproof vest but others striking him in the head. He fell on his side and began screaming in pain. His cries were pitiful, unbearable. The gendarmes redoubled their fire so as not to hear them and to avenge their leader, and they were spurred on by Goémond's megaphone. The commissioner fell back slightly with his deputies, aligning with the gendarmes' left flank. Meanwhile the radio operator crawled over on his belly to the wounded officer. He turned him on his back, which only worsened the man's horrible screams. Taking him beneath the arms, he hauled him out of the anarchists' line of fire. The officer passed out, and his wailing ceased.

Buenaventura, his left arm throbbing with pain, reached the foot of the stairs on all fours. The front windows shattered and tumbled like broken chandeliers. The other detachment of gendarmes, positioned in front of the house, had joined the action following their orders. Their rounds peppered the back wall and the staircase. An empty beer bottle on the table exploded.

"Is there anyone down here?" shouted Buenaventura.

"Yes," replied Épaulard from the kitchen, but his voice was too weak for the Catalan to hear it.

"Launch grenades!" ordered Goémond in a resounding voice. "Smoke the rats out of their hole."

Plunk! went the gas grenade launchers. Two projectiles passed through the kitchen window and bounced on the tiles.

"My back must be broken," said Épaulard with his lips touching the floor. "I can't move my arms and legs. Don't come to get me; you couldn't move me in any case."

He did not know whether anyone could hear him. Then the two grenades exploded. They were nonlethal, producing only a limited shock wave and dispersing CS gas. Épaulard's body jerked and his sides, legs and back were struck by shrapnel. He began to cough with difficulty. The kitchen was full of gas, which escaped rather slowly through the window.

Buenaventura was crouching at the foot of the stairs. He felt his left arm and found the entry hole in his sweater made by the bullet. He pushed a finger through and tore the garment open from there to the exit hole so that he could examine the wound. His punctured biceps was already swollen and purple, oozing blood and hurting like the devil.

Someone began running down the stairs.

"Don't come down here!" cried Buenaventura.

Meyer paid not the slightest attention to this injunction. The cops at the front kept up their fire. As he reached the sixth step Meyer took a round in the heart. He sat down on the stairs, dead, then slithered the rest of the way. He landed on top of Buenaventura.

"Are you hit, Meyer? Have you been hit?" the Catalan asked Meyer's corpse.

Upstairs, Cash was no longer firing because she could not free an empty magazine from her weapon. She had seen Meyer emerge hotfoot from the ambassador's room.

"That's enough of that!" he had shouted as he passed her. "We're fucked. I'm going to give myself up! I have a wife!"

He had then disappeared. Cash looked at the door to the room he had left. She wondered whether Meyer had left his pistol behind in his excitement. She wondered where Épaulard was. She wondered if Buenaventura was wounded. She wondered what D'Arcy was doing.

Grenades launched by the police squad at the front of the house reached the common area and the three upstairs bedrooms and exploded. Cash heard a cry from the ambassador's room, then the diplomat came out in his undershorts, pro ͏e with one hand, the other hand empty.

͏ot me, I beg of you," he cried, as she pointed ͏n at him.

"Okay. Lie down on your belly by the wall, you fat bastard. And don't move."

"You people ought to surrender," said the ambassador. "You must see that you are helpless. They haven't the slightest intention of negotiating with you."

"Shut up!"

At the foot of the stairs, Buenaventura took advantage of the clouds of gas that now filled the common area. He grabbed Meyer's automatic and took his chances. He rushed up the staircase without being hit and found himself upstairs. Cash aimed her Sten at Buenaventura before recognizing him. The ambassador was lying prone alongside the wall. Buenaventura's face was as white as a sheet. Blood flowed down over his left hand and dripped onto the floorboards.

"Buen, what's the matter with you?" asked Cash. Then she yelled, "What are you doing?"

The Catalan shoved her aside, knelt on one knee near Richard Poindexter and put a single round in his head. Cash screeched out in disgust. The back of the ambassador's skull was shattered, his hair powder-burnt, and his blood was seeping onto the floor around his face. Buenaventura stood up. He looked at Cash, who remained motionless, eyes wide, tight-mouthed from nausea.

"They're shooting to kill," said the Catalan. "They came to slaughter, not arrest us."

He looked thoughtful.

"That makes one less diplomat, at least," he added distractedly.

Cash threw her Sten down on the floor.

"I'm going to surrender."

"Don't do it. They'll kill you."

Cash remained still, leaning against the wall, her mind

blank. The Catalan picked up her submachine gun, removed the jammed magazine and replaced it with another.

Grenades kept on coming in through the broken windows and exploding very loudly in the bedrooms and on the ground floor. The gas spread into the upstairs hallway as clouds of it emerged from the bedrooms near the stairs.

"Where is Épaulard? Where is D'Arcy?" asked Buenaventura.

He had to repeat his query on account of the racket and on account of Cash's inattention.

"D'Arcy is in the garage," said the girl. "Épaulard—where is Épaulard?"

"That's what I'm asking you!"

"He went down. He's below."

Cash turned and headed for the stairs.

"Don't go down there! We can get into the garage by breaking through the roof. Cash!"

The girl took three quick strides and took off down the stairs, disappearing into the clouds of gas. Buenaventura saw no more of her; he merely heard her coughing.

"Well, shit!" he groaned. "And long live death."

Sticking the automatic into his pants pocket and the Sten under his right arm, he ran to the end of the hallway, to the end of the main building. With his left arm he executed a rapid piston-like motion to prevent it from seizing up. The pain was acute, and the bleeding from his perforated muscle increased.

Cash got to the foot of the staircase coughing. The firing had ceased. Meyer's body lay by the bottom stair. Cash stepped over it, still coughing, and made for the back door, which was open, and there she came face-to-face with Goémond, two of his deputies and a gendarme armed with a submachine gun. The four men wore gas masks and stared at her through a green and white cloud of chlorobenzalmalo-nonitrile, also known as CS gas.

"I surrender," said Cash, coughing and raising her hands above her head.

Goémond put a bullet in her chest. The girl was thrown backwards by the impact. She fell supine in the middle of the common area.

"You," said Goémond to the gendarme, "you will forget what you just saw. Think of your pension."

He strode to the doorway of the kitchen. He glanced inside and saw Épaulard flat on his face in the room. He signaled the other men to proceed. Moving in fits and starts, the three cops went and hunkered down at the foot of the stairs. The gendarme then let fly with a burst of fire up into the fog as the two policemen rapidly clambered up the staircase.

Goémond went into the kitchen. He leant over Épaulard, who was retching spasmodically. He grabbed his hair and pulled his head up. The eyes of the injured man were red and swollen, and his whole face was purplish.

"Don't touch me," he murmured. "My back's broken."

Goémond let the fifty-year-old's head fall back down, and then, slipping his foot under the man's torso, he gave a good shove and turned him over. Épaulard squeaked like a mouse and his tongue came out of his mouth. Goémond felt for a pulse and then stood up straight, satisfied.

Upstairs, Buenaventura had entered the bathroom and pointlessly locked the door behind him. He had broken through the ceiling and torn away the sections of insulation and tar paper that separated him from the tiles of the roof. Standing on the bathtub, he carefully pushed up one of those tiles to survey the surroundings. He was at the northern extremity of the main building, whose roof adjoined that of the north wing (under which was the garage). Indeed, had Buenaventura had the requisite tools, he could have knocked through the bathroom wall above the tub and so reached the garage directly.

From this vantage point, the garage's roof was at the center of his visual field. To the right he could see the countryside. From that side no assault had been made, for the farmhouse had no opening that way. Gendarmes were nevertheless to be seen, a small squad crouched in a grove of trees about a hundred meters away.

To the left, Buenaventura's line of sight passed between the two wings of the farmstead and over the muddy terrain that separated it from the byroad. There a considerable body of gendarmes was visible. The men had ceased firing, either because they had received an order or because there was no further riposte from the farm. They appeared to be awaiting the order to advance.

The Catalan held his submachine gun horizontally before him and gave a good push with it. Fifteen or so tiles shifted and tumbled away. The young man swiftly hoisted himself through, rolled over and slid on his belly down the slope of the roof. He ended up at the opposite sloping roof over the garage and at once began frantically wrenching tiles from it. He was now in plain view of the gendarmes massed on the byroad as well as of those hunkered down in the grove of trees to the north.

"Hey! You there on the roof!" came a shout from a megaphone. "Put your hands up and don't move! Or we'll shoot!"

Back inside the farmhouse, Goémond, having just finished off Épaulard, heard and mentally cursed the gendarmerie officer for giving someone a chance to escape with their life.

Buenaventura ripped up three more tiles and dived through the hole he had made without being shot. He found himself on a wooden platform that extended only partway over the ground floor of this wing of the farm, originally serving agricultural purposes. For the most part, nothing came between the dirt floor and the roof six meters above, which was supported by ancient beams. The Catalan was in a former hayloft that the owner of the farm had recently decided to convert into a mezzanine. He approached the edge of the platform and in the half darkness of the place saw the green Jaguar down below with its motor running, the door open, and D'Arcy sitting in the driver's seat with his legs dangling out of the car, drinking from a liter bottle of red wine.

The alcoholic held a pistol in his other hand and as he continued to drink his gaze was fixed on Buenaventura.

"It's me," said the Catalan.

D'Arcy detached the bottle from his lips.

"So I see," he said. "What's happening? Where do we stand?"

A ladder led down from the hayloft to the earthen floor. Buenaventura climbed down.

"They're all dead, I guess," he said as he completed his descent. "I killed the ambassador. We're completely surrounded, and we can't even surrender."

D'Arcy emptied his bottle and threw it against a wall. It shattered.

"Fine," he said. "Let's die. Let's go for broke."

"Long live death!" said Buenaventura again.

He walked around the Jaguar, opened the passenger door and climbed in. With the barrel of the Sten he smashed the windshield and cleared away the fragments of glass still clinging to the frame. D'Arcy slammed the driver's door.

"Directly opposite the exit," said the alcoholic, "is the byroad we came in on the other evening. I'm stepping on it. We won't make it."

"Okay."

"Goodbye, you old shithead."

"Goodbye."

The Jaguar came out of the garage, slowly because it needed to turn right away, then sped towards the exit barrier.

The gendarmes were busy opening the gate and getting ready to move forward. They were taken by surprise as much as they could be, which is to say not very much.

Stuffed down into his seat, his torso jammed against the wheel and his eyes just above the top of the dashboard, D'Arcy accelerated madly. Buenaventura, resting the Sten's barrel on the rim of the broken windshield, sprayed the way ahead with bullets and emptied the magazine before the car reached the gate. Many of the gendarmes scattered frantically, diving into the ditches and kicking up snow and mud all around them. Others, some armed with Mousquetons, some with submachine guns, opened fire on the Jaguar in a disorderly but effective way. The vehicle was peppered with bullets.

"The tires!" yelled an officer at the top of his voice.

The Jaguar passed through the gate, crossed the byroad and roared onto a tractor track that led off along the side of a little wooded valley. The car's side windows were blown to smithereens on the way. The fire from the guardians of the law died down. The tires had been shredded. Holes had been punched in the rear bodywork.

D'Arcy had taken two rounds in the chest, one in the neck, and one in his side. He let go of the wheel and collapsed onto it, nose pointing ahead and arms dangling. Blood spurted from his carotid artery in great sporadic surges. His foot was jammed on the gas pedal.

The Jag gathered speed fast as it went down the track, failed to turn at a bend, uprooted bushes, and veered off to the side into a deep gully that served as a public garbage dump. It rolled over three times amid the trash before crashing at the bottom of the hollow and coming to a halt.

Buenaventura found himself on all fours in the refuse without knowing how he got there. Just as he was contemplating the motionless car some twenty meters further down, its doors open, its tires flat, its roof caved in, its hood gone, it caught fire. First the gas tank spewed a great sinuous flame, then the engine was ablaze, and finally the tank exploded and a plume of smoke and debris rose into the air above the hollow. The Catalan began to run straight ahead along the hillside, continually losing his footing.

On the byroad the astounded cops could no longer see the automobile. It had vanished beyond the bend down the tractor track and was now burning and exploding lower down, out of their line of sight. The officer detached a dozen of his men to investigate, and they left at a run, hunched over their weapons.

When they came within sight of the burning wreck, the Catalan had already disappeared into the shady thickets at the far end of the gully. He had found a path that paralleled the departmental road to Couzy. He ran as fast as his legs could carry him. The terrain was wooded. The fugitive was invisible. He came to a turn. Buenaventura emerged onto the departmental road. Couzy was half a kilometer away, but at less than fifty meters there was a small BP gas station. Buenaventura continued running along the main road. He was wheezing badly. He felt very weak and light-headed. His arm was still bleeding. He had sprained his right ankle. He went on running.

On the forecourt of the garage an old Peugeot 203 pickup was being gassed up. Its owner, in blue overalls, was chatting with the pump attendant, a fat, jolly lad, hands black with oil. The Catalan stumbled over to the two and took his automatic from his pocket.

"Fill her up," he said. "Don't move."

Neither man moved. The attendant went on filling the gas tank. Buenaventura leant his shoulder against the 203.

"Is it my truck you want?" asked the man in blue overalls in a stricken voice.

"Yes."

The man tried to chuckle but only managed to choke.

"It's not worth anything," he said. "It's a clunker."

"Listen," said Buenaventura, "I'm the only survivor of Nada, the anarchist group that kidnapped the American Ambassador on Friday night. The police tracked us down at a farm near here and killed my comrades in cold blood. Do you understand what I'm telling you?"

"You mean those anarchists who snatched the American Ambassador!"

"Listen," said Buenaventura wearily, "and try to remember. You can tell this to the press. You'll have your photo in the paper . . . The police massacred us. The cops killed everyone at the farm. And the ambassador was killed because the cops would not let us give ourselves up. Do you get that?"

"Who killed him, the ambassador?" asked the pump attendant.

"What a fucking idiot!" sighed the Catalan.

The car was filled up. The attendant removed the nozzle of his pump. He replaced the gas cap.

"Turn around, both of you," ordered Buenaventura.

The two men turned around. The Catalan brought the barrel of his pistol down on the skull of the man in blue overalls, who cried out in pain and collapsed. The attendant took to his heels. He fled towards the garage office. Buenaventura suppressed an urge to shoot at him and leapt into the 203. He started up, turned the truck around and headed in the direction of Paris. From the door of his office the garage attendant fired at the pickup with a single-shot Simplex, and a scatter of number 7 shot riddled the vehicle. The Catalan accelerated. The 203 disappeared around a bend. It was twenty-five past ten in the morning. The mayhem had lasted less than half an hour.

# 33

THE NEWS came over the radio in the late morning and gave rise to a brief special bulletin that was expanded and commented on at lunchtime, notably on television, where images appeared of "the tragic farmhouse," the broken glass on the tiled floor, the ambassador's coagulated blood, and the wrecked Jaguar. Pronouncements and cabled messages multiplied. Condolences of the French government to the ambassador's widow, to the U.S. government. Communiqué from the minister of the interior announcing that order had been restored, taking credit for this, but at the same time warning everyone to be on guard against any recurrence of such excesses and hastening not to overlook the need to pay respectful homage to the memory of Richard Poindexter. Telegram from the Holy Father to the President of the Republic. Message from the Archbishop of Paris. Telegram from the prime minister to the family of the gendarmerie officer currently fighting for his life in a hospital bed. Congratulatory telegram from the minister of armies to the mobile gendarmerie group deployed at Couzy. Proclamation of a group of Bordigist militants denouncing law enforcement for opening fire without due warning on the farmhouse and thus being solely responsible for the death of the ambassador (a proclamation that almost prompted the minister of armies to bring defamation charges). Confidential message from the commander of the accused mobile gendarmerie force to the director of gendarmerie and military justice lodging a specific formal complaint against Commissioner Goémond (subsequent to which the minister of armies would abandon any defamation charges and request an urgent meeting with the minister of the interior). Communiqué from the Organisation Révolutionnaire Libertaire (ORL), a clandestine organization composed of twelve members, four of them undercover police agents, calling upon all revolutionaries to kill "at least fifty cops" to avenge the comrades killed at Couzy. Statement of Independent Union of Otorhinolaryngologists informing the public that ORLs had nothing to do with the above-mentioned organization. Etc., etc., etc.

A team of medical examiners was preparing a set of autopsy reports, but in the mind of the public the chain of events was already as clear as day. Surrounded, the terrorists, rather than surrendering, had preferred to kill their hostage and open fire on law enforcement, who had laid siege to the house. André Épaulard ("a strange kind of international adventurer"), Nathan Meyer ("a waiter described by his coworkers as an aggressive and unbalanced introvert"), and Véronique Cash ("the group's Pasionaria") had all been killed, weapons in hand, during the police operation. Benoît D'Arcy, "scion of an alcoholic and degenerate family," had been neutralized moments later as he broke through a barrier at the wheel of an expensive sports car and fired on the police. Buenaventura Diaz, "undoubtedly the most dangerous, a veteran anarchist with no visible means of support," had managed to make a getaway and was being actively sought. Television broadcast his picture. He had the pale face of a scrawny thug with long hair and eyes terrifying enough to make respectable people shake in their shoes.

# 34

BUENAVENTURA was looking at his likeness on the television screen.

In the Peugeot 203 pickup, he had reached the Morin Valley and cruised unknown roads indecisively. After an hour he drove the vehicle into a quarry. What kind of quarry, the Catalan did not know, but the fact was that yellowish, somewhat clayey walls rose like ramparts around an area covered by large puddles of water where mud-streaked orange trucks stood dormant alongside rails and rusty quarry tubs. An iron-gray work-site shed, prefabricated, was in one corner. After parking the 203 behind a truck out of sight of the main road, Buenaventura broke open the door of the shed with the help of a crowbar. He was hot, he was cold, he sweated, he shivered. Inside the shed he came upon an empty cot, a desk, plastic hard hats, yellow oilskins, an opened liter bottle of wine, piles of documents, and a Vélosolex moped. He had struck lucky.

Buenaventura lingered for a while inside the shed. The quarry would probably remain deserted until Monday morning, but it was a precarious hideaway. Furthermore, there would be dances in the valley, and couples could easily drive up here eager to make out and then spot the 203, which had certainly been reported stolen by now.

Since his wound continued to bleed sporadically, the

Catalan applied a compression bandage composed of a dirty rag and a bungee cord. He slipped back into his dark sweater with its ripped sleeve stiff with blood. He felt very feeble. He drank a little wine and immediately threw up. He staggered. He wiped his chin and forehead with the back of his right hand, clumsily donned a yellow oilskin, and took the moped outside.

The machine's motor would not start. Buenaventura was unfamiliar with its operation. As much as he jiggled with every part that seemed jigglable, the engine would not come to life. Perhaps the bike had broken down. The Catalan resigned himself to pedaling despite his greatly weakened state. He returned to the road, zigzagging, comfortable on the downhill, struggling on the up, and striving to put a good distance between himself and the 203.

Thanks to the snow and the weekend's dismal damp weather, the traffic was not heavy. The odd car came towards him or overtook him, but for the moment no one paid attention to the Catalan.

Eventually he left the road and went up a broad driveway leading to an isolated house. It had a lugubrious villa-like aspect and stood amid trees in a square clearing with a meticulously laid-out and maintained rock garden in front of it and grass behind and on either side. It appeared to be a weekend place, and it was closed up. Buenaventura gained access by first entering the garage (breaking a frosted-glass window) and then forcing the communicating door between the garage and the living quarters. He emerged into a small foyer with a tiled floor, opened the nearest door and found himself in a stolid living room with fake country-style furniture. A portable television sat on the floor tiles at the far end. Buenaventura consulted his watch, which had stopped at ten twenty-three. He walked over to the television and turned it on. When the screen lit up, he saw himself.

# 35

ALL DAY Sunday myriads of identity checks were made across the department of Seine-et-Marne, as also in Paris, where fresh raids were mounted in known leftist circles. On Boulevard de la Chapelle a small, more or less spontaneous demonstration, accompanied by chants of "Goémond Is a Rat!" and the time-honored "The People Will Have Your Hide!" was dispersed, but skirmishes continued throughout the evening. Meanwhile, some Jewish shops were looted by Kabyles, and a Malian pimp was wounded by a revolver shot. At Place de l'Étoile, other demonstrators, from the New Order movement, were pushed back to Avenue Hoche, which they marched down shouting "Democracy stinks!" An orator from the ultrarightist Action Française Nationale Révolutionnaire, who referred bizarrely to the terrorists as "our strayed comrades," was bludgeoned by the New Order militants.

# 36

BUENAVENTURA saw no need to stay on watch. He had turned the television off. He went and opened the back door of the weekend house and brought his moped inside, safe from hypothetical eyes. Then he looked for the bathroom, found it, and ran himself a bath. The pilot of the oil-fired heater was on and he had hot water. He undressed but winced as he did so. His arm was stiff and painful. He undid the dressing to examine his wound. His biceps was black and red. A good anarchist's biceps, he thought with a chuckle that curled his lip.

Opening the medicine cabinet, he found ether, which he splashed liberally over the muscle. The bathroom whirled around him. He slumped into a sitting position against the bathtub, and a great chill ran through him. Was this death? he wondered in a rush of unfettered romanticism. It was not death; it was just the ether. The Catalan got to his feet and hopped about, as his injury burned. Then the pain subsided. He slipped into the water, making sure to soak his left arm. With his right hand he poked about in his clothing, which he had tossed onto a wooden stool by the tub. As his body relaxed in the warm water, he lit a twisted and crushed Gauloise and smoked it contentedly. Ashes fell into the bathwater.

He stayed still for a while, his face hardened by thought or by something else that hardened his face.

Then he grabbed his automatic pistol and awkwardly removed the magazine. He had fired only once, so seven shots were left, and he had no spare ammo. He replaced the magazine with a round in the chamber, got out of the water, splashing a good deal of it on the tiled floor. He dried himself, though not properly, using just one hand. He then went back to the tub, plunged his head in the dirty water and pulled it out drenched. Taking a pair of barber's scissors from the medicine cabinet, he set about trimming his wet mop of hair. He finished the job with a Gillette razor and shaving cream from an aerosol can, but no brush. Playfully, he sprayed a circle in shaving cream on the mirror.

When he returned to the living room he was barefoot and wearing an old dressing gown with his automatic in the pocket. His hair was more or less closely cropped and combed. He had shaved the nape of his neck and face (without avoiding nicks), but left a sort of *mouche*, not very thick, indeed little more than three days' growth of beard, beneath his lower lip. He had also shaved part of his eyebrows in hopes of altering his look, but the result was merely bizarre and liable to attract attention. In his wake he left damp footprints on the tiles. He felt cold. He found the heating thermostat in the foyer and set it for twenty degrees.

He now explored the house. Upstairs, in a bedroom armoire, he found something to wear, weekend gear suitable for a middle manager: corduroy pants and a white turtleneck sweater stretchy enough for the sleeve to accommodate the gauze and Albuplast-tape dressing that Buenaventura had contrived on getting out of the bath. The Catalan also took a green-and-blue-checked hunting jacket with leather elbow patches. All these clothes were rather large for him, and the pants ballooned at the seat, but when you were an assassin, a fugitive, a hunted animal, you could not have everything.

As he toured the weekend house, the hunted animal began growling, then the growl changed into a song, an old song, silly and meaningless, a waltz:

*Il m'a dit, "Voulez-vous danser?"*
*J'ai dit oui presque sans penser.*

He asked me, "Would you like to dance?"
I said yes almost without thinking.

Still singing, Buenaventura went back down to the ground floor. He left the lights on everywhere behind the closed shutters as he passed through.

*Il m'a dit, "Voulez-vous danser?"*

The Catalan entered a rather masculine office and addressed a mirror on the wall that reflected his bizarre appearance.

"Paris must be made to dance!" he roared.

He turned away and went around a dark worktable. His eyes were alight.

"When it comes to making Paris dance, we've had it, buddy," he declared with irony.

He stationed himself in front of a gun rack containing two firearms—a shotgun and a carbine. He took each down in turn to check them out: a Model H Charlin shotgun with two break-action barrels, which he broke and then reclosed; and an Erma .22 midsize lever-action long rifle.

"A foretaste of what is to come," grumbled Buenaventura as he put the guns back in the rack.

They did not interest him much anymore.

"*Ya se van los pastores a la Estremadura,*" he started to sing in falsetto.

"You dumb fuck of a shitty fake Spaniard!" he shouted as he passed the mirror again on his way out of the office.

He was hungry. He went into the kitchen, opened a can of cassoulet and scoffed it with a teaspoon. It was cold. It was greasy. It was disgusting. He drank cheap red wine from a bottle broken off at the neck and a label reading "Estate bottled especially for MONSIEUR VENTRÉE."

His hunger assuaged, the Catalan went back into the living room and paced up and down for a few more minutes. His head was heavy. He was irritated. There was not a single fucking radio in this shithouse, in Monsieur Ventrée's crappy Ali Baba's cave. Then he had an idea. He returned to the kind of office, where there was a telephone. He dialed INF 1, but all he got by way of response were jumbled sounds and a distinctly unmusical dial tone. There had to be a lousy regional prefix to enter. Buenaventura was damned if he was going to look it up in the phone book. He went back into the living room and turned the TV on. *The Bridges at Toko-Ri* was playing, a stupid film about the Korean War. The Catalan sat down in an armchair in front of the set and passed out from all the blood he had lost.

When he came to, the admiral played by Fredric March was confiding in Grace Kelly about his wife, who had taken a big hit on account of their son having been wiped out by the Reds.

"She sits quietly alone in her room knitting a baby's sweater," said the admiral dolefully.

"She'd do better to go get laid," observed Buenaventura as he muted the sound.

He went directly back to the office, wobbling a little.

On the dark wooden table, a small electric clock encased in a solid greenish crystalline block—probably solidified shit—indicated that it was almost six in the evening, and it was true that there was no longer any daylight outside the windows. Buenaventura swore and hastily circulated through the house turning off all the lights. Returning to the office holding a small box flashlight, he opened a drawer in search of paper. He found instead a cheap little tape recorder that took minicassettes.

"That's even better," he said in the semidarkness.

He delved deeper into the drawer, which was full of mini-cassettes. He took one out at random. It had a handwritten label: *Joël at three months.*

"Joël can go and get fucked!" said Buenaventura. "You can all go and get fucked!"

He inserted the cassette into the recorder, made sure the batteries were sufficiently charged, attached the microphone, hit Record and dictated a complete account of the abduction of the ambassador and the siege of the farmhouse. To authenticate his testimony he supplied the serial number and provenance of the automatic used to kill the ambassador.

He searched for an envelope, found one, slipped the cassette into it, and sealed it.

On the envelope he wrote the address of a press agency. He looked for stamps but found none. Okay. He would see to that later. He put the package in the pocket of his hunting jacket. He wanted very much to smoke but had no more cigarettes. He turned the office and the living room completely upside down without finding any tobacco. He sat down again, took the recorder and stuck in another minicassette, this one labeled *The Marriage of Maryse*.

"So she finally did go and get fucked," remarked Buenaventura, whose train of thought was increasingly disordered.

He grasped the mike, pressed Record, and as the tape began to roll he stayed still for a moment with his mouth open and his face hardened as it had been in the early afternoon in the bathtub.

"I made a mistake," he said abruptly. "Leftist terrorism and State terrorism, even if their motivations cannot be compared, are the two jaws of..."

He hesitated.

"...of the same mug's game," he concluded, and went on right away: "The regime defends itself, naturally, against terrorism. But the system does not defend itself against it. It encourages it and publicizes it. The desperado is a commodity, an exchange value, a model of behavior like a cop or a female saint. The State's dream is a horrific, triumphant finale to an absolutely general civil war to the death between cohorts of cops and mercenaries on the one hand and nihilistic armed groups on the other. This vision is the trap laid for rebels, and I fell into it. And I won't be the last. And that pisses me off in the worst way."

The Catalan stared into the shadows and mechanically rubbed his mouth with his hand. He had a vision of his father, whom he had never seen. The man was on a barricade, or more precisely in the process of stepping over it, with one leg up in the air; it was the evening of May 4, 1937, in Barcelona, and the revolutionary proletariat had risen against the bourgeoisie and the Stalinists. In a fraction of a second a bullet was going to strike Buenaventura's father, and in a fraction of a second he would be dead, while in a few days the Barcelona Commune would be crushed and very soon its memory would be buried in calumny.

"The condemnation of terrorism," Buenaventura said into the mike, "is not a condemnation of insurrection but a call to insurrection."

He interrupted himself once more, and a snicker twisted his lips.

"Consequently," he added, "I pronounce the Nada group dissolved."

He stopped recording.

"And with unanimous support yet again!" he shouted in the darkness. "The old traditions must be respected."

He took the cassette from the recorder, thrust it into another envelope, which he closed and on which he wrote: *First and Last Theoretical Contribution of Buenaventura Diaz to His Own History.* He put the envelope into the pocket of the hunting jacket and went into the living room to get the television news.

"Commissioner Goémond, the man who this morning led the assault intended to free the U.S. Ambassador," began a newscaster even before the policeman's image appeared on the screen. Then, as Goémond's head and shoulders materialized, he went on: "and I offer this information with strict reservations, based on a dispatch just in: Commissioner Goémond, has thus reportedly—and I stress 'reportedly'—been suspended on direct orders from the minister of the interior."

"Well," said Buenaventura, "if that isn't something else."

# 37

"You can't do that!" objected Goémond.

"Sure I can, Goémond. Who do you think you are?" replied the chief of staff.

"I acted on your instructions."

"Your name has been chanted in the streets of Paris," said the chief of staff. "They are shouting 'Goémond is a swine' and 'Today's pig is tomorrow's bacon.'"

"Those are death threats."

"Stop talking nonsense, Goémond."

"Very well then, let me talk some sense," answered Goémond in a toneless voice. "Do you really think this is a time to expose yourself to scandal by firing me?"

"You are not fired. You are suspended."

"Answer my question!" shouted Goémond.

"If I care to, I will!" yelled back the chief of staff, rising from his chair red in the face. "Goémond, really, you would be well advised to back off! Do you understand me, commissioner? Just back off! And sit down!"

Goémond sat down and held his tongue. His interlocutor strode angrily up and down the office.

"For some time now, commissioner, you've been putting too much stock in yourself. Perhaps you think you're above the law? You conducted this operation with a brutality that cannot and will not be tolerated. You took it upon yourself…"

"Upon myself?"

"Be quiet. You are in no position to interrupt me. You took it upon yourself to order an assault on the farmhouse even though you knew full well that this was liable to cost the ambassador his life. You let yourself be swayed by pre-judicial impulses, Goémond, by a sick passion. You're verging on psychosis, Goémond! I remember your own words: 'If it were just up to me, I'd put them up against the wall.'"

"I don't remember *your* own words," said the commissioner in a strained voice, "but I do know what I understood."

"Not another word, Goémond!" said the chief of staff. "I have no time for your fantasies!"

The commissioner's lips moved silently for a moment, then he calmed down. He took several deep breaths. The chief of staff had stopped pacing and was looking at him with a probing expression.

"All right," sighed Goémond. "So I'm the scapegoat."

"I'd be grateful if you refrained from using that absurd and tendentious word after you leave this office," said the chief of staff, and he pursed his lips.

"Grateful to what degree?"

The chief of staff went behind his desk and sat down. He lit a Gitane Filtre and contemplated Goémond through the smoke, blinking.

"Very likely disciplinary measures will have to be taken, I have to tell you," he said. "A spell away won't do you any harm. You will be going to provide technical assistance to the niggers."

"With the niggers!" exclaimed Goémond with a nervous shudder.

"Somewhere in Africa, yes, which wouldn't be a bad solu-tion. If you have sadistic tendencies, you can give them free rein out there. Anyway, we'll see. It's not up to me, you realize."

Goémond said nothing. The chief of staff shrugged.

"I'm sorry about this," he said. "But things have been building up. There was the suicide attempt of the Meyer woman. The complaints of the gendarmes, you know how they are . . . For the public the whole episode reeks of brutality, and even the Americans noticed. I've had the Foreign Office on the line. A shit storm, if you'll excuse the expression. Anyway, in a word, there it is."

The chief of staff got back to his feet, signaling that the interview had gone on long enough. Goémond got up too, red faced, eyes bulging, mustache aquiver. He held himself in check.

"Try to make sure you grab that last anarchist," he said huskily. "If he opens his trap, the shit will really hit the fan."

"Goodbye, Goémond," said the chief of staff. "You have permission to go to your office and deal with pending matters and hand things off. Then it's back home for you, Goémond. Understand? Bed rest!"

"Goodbye," said Goémond, and left.

The night air struck his sweaty skin like a cold shower. He walked hesitantly to his car. He got in and sat motionless, his hands tight on the steering wheel, staring into space. The commissioner was a broken man for just over thirty seconds. Then he knew what he still had to do (the idea struck him like a thunderbolt) if he was to take his revenge. He started up and headed at speed for his office.

When he entered the room where Treuffais was handcuffed to the radiator, the philosophy teacher raised his head feebly. His eyes were deep hollows. Goémond drew his blackjack from his inside pocket and struck Treuffais in the head. The young man closed his eyes, his jaw dropped open, and he toppled over alongside the wall.

Two deputies had come in behind the commissioner.

"Take him out by the door to the courtyard and put him in my car," ordered Goémond. "In five or ten minutes, start off and go and wait for me at his address."

"Boss," said the younger of the policemen, "are you sure you know what you are doing? I mean . . . Why not drop it?"

"Why?" cried Goémond, and his cry sounded like a cat yowling. "Why!" he repeated, more softly this time, and he left the room shrugging and repeating the word in an amused tone.

Downstairs, he waited for a moment or two to give the journalists, tipped off by a calculated leak, time to gather, then left the building to be met on the sidewalk by popping flashbulbs that lit up the night, mikes held out and questions hurled. Dazzled, Goémond elbowed his way through the crowd like a Hugolian oarsman.

"Let me pass. Gangway, gangway. Come on."

He reached the black Citroën DS that he had had brought to the front entrance. He turned back to the mob assailing him.

"I have only one thing to say. Only one thing!" he shouted above the racket. "They want to scapegoat me, but with the ambassador business I was strictly obeying orders."

He sniggered. The questions redoubled. People were pushing and shoving to get closer to him. Trampling one another. Goémond reveled in his power. Once again sweat began trickling down his sickly broad brow.

"And another thing!" he yelled. "We had known since last month about the intended abduction of the U.S. Ambassador. I had an informant inside the Nada group. He didn't take part in the final preparations for the job, but until the beginning of the week he was aware of what the anarchists were planning. He did not know the exact date of the attack, but that's the only thing he didn't know."

Go ahead and sort that lot out, thought Goémond, picturing the face of the chief of staff when it got back to him.

"Yes, yes!" he shouted to the journalists. "And this informant is alive. He is free. But no, I can't reveal his identity."

But Buenaventura Diaz could, he thought, and he felt jubilant as he opened the door of the DS, climbed in, and slammed the door. He started the engine.

"No, I have no further comment!"

He rolled up the window. The DS drew away from the curb, drew away from the crowd, and raced off on the wet roadway onto which the streetlamps were projecting ghostly patches of light.

It was nearly eleven at night when the commissioner reached Treuffais's street. A small street. There were no passersby. His Renault 15 was double-parked. Goémond pulled up right behind it and got out. One of the deputies was waiting in the Renault's driver's seat. The other was in the back beside the unconscious Treuffais.

"Help me get him up to his place," said Goémond.

Once they were in the apartment, Goémond stretched Treuffais out on the living-room floor.

"Off you go, guys. I don't need you now."

"Boss, please let me stay with you," said the younger deputy.

"Out of the question. But would you mind doing me another favor?"

The commissioner took off his jacket and handed it to his subordinates.

"Take my car to Bercy or thereabouts," he said, "and leave it in a place where it causes an obstruction. On an expressway entrance ramp, for instance. Leave my jacket on the front seat and spread my papers around on top of it, my ID, okay, and all that..."

"That will attract attention."

"That's exactly what I want, dodo. It will keep the cops occupied for a while," said the police commissioner.

"Okay."

"One more thing: drag things out as much as you can."

"Okay."

"See you later, lads."

"Knock on wood," said the younger deputy.

# 38

WHEN A nighttime television bulletin conveyed the news, quoting Commissioner Goémond's statements with all due reservations, it took Buenaventura, who was eating pâté and drinking cognac in front of the set, a few seconds to realize what the policeman was up to. Then:

"That son of a bitch!" he declared loudly.

For a moment or two he did not move. Then he finished his cognac and went into the garage. On entering the house he had noticed a workbench there. The Catalan poked around among the tools and found what he reckoned he needed. Flashlight in one hand, three saws in the other, he went back into the house and returned to the office. He sawed for some two hours. He was in no hurry. He was thinking, and he was weak. He took care not to reopen his wound with sudden movements.

When he had finished sawing, he had at his disposal, on the one hand, the Charlin shotgun reduced to its simplest form, thirty-five centimeters long with stripped-down butt and barrels, and on the other hand the Erma carbine rifle in a broadly similar state, though a little longer and very reminiscent of the Mare's Leg—the shortened Winchester beloved by Steve McQueen in the TV series *Wanted: Dead or Alive.*

The anarchist stuffed his pockets with twelve-gauge shotgun shells and loaded the carbine mag with .22 long rifle ammo. He went back upstairs and managed to find an enormous floppy khaki trench coat with two inside pockets. He cut off the bottoms of the pockets with scissors. He then slid in the two sawed-off guns, one on each side, so that they fitted neatly within the coat's lining and hung down more or less vertically. He put the trench coat on over his hunting jacket. Weighed down now by several extra kilos, with his automatic pistol in the inside pocket of the jacket, he descended to the ground floor, turned the television off by hitting it with a chair, and left the house by the back door, wheeling his Solex moped.

"Death to the pigs!" he declared fervently as he straddled the bike.

With no light save for the box flashlight, he traveled slowly by back roads. Coming to a sleeping populated area, he smashed a window on a Fiat 128, got into the car, started it up without too much trouble, and set off again.

He succeeded in reaching Paris without running into any roadblocks, without encountering any obstacles to his plans. It felt was as though he had managed to trick fate.

He left the ring road at Porte de la Plaine, headed into the city, and parked on Boulevard Lefebvre. Sitting in the front of the Fiat, he took a break. He was humming.

The building must be locked up, he trilled to the tune of *Il m'a dit, "Voulez-vous danser?"*

He got out of the car. The cognac had the delayed effect of accelerating his heartbeat. Leaning against the Fiat, he withdrew the Erma awkwardly from the right-hand lining of his coat. His left arm hurt unrelentingly, but no more than it would have with a wooden peg driven through the muscle.

He took the sawed-off carbine in his right hand and slid the remnants of its butt up his sleeve until not much of the weapon was visible. His left hand held the automatic pistol. Thus prepared, he set off, tottering like a drunk. He expected that he would soon run into cops posted around Treuffais's hideaway. His intention, crazily, was to kill them all and force his way through to his friend. He was surprised not to encounter anyone before reaching the end of the block. The cops must be right inside the building, also no doubt on the roof, just waiting for him to fall into the crude trap set for him by Goémond.

# 39

"YOU ARE completely mad," said Treuffais.

"No."

"Do you intend to wait here for long?"

"Two days. Three days. As long as it takes."

Treuffais shook his head. He was handcuffed all over again to a radiator. He was sitting on the floor with his back to the wall of his seedy living room. Commissioner Goémond was ensconced in the father's armchair in his shirtsleeves; he was wearing a bulletproof vest, with his service pistol in a shoulder holster and a Colt Cobra on his knees. The kitchen light was on and it shed a yellow rectangle on the living-room floor. On either side of this rectangle sat Treuffais and Goémond looking at each other in the half darkness of the room. The prisoner was in a state of great fatigue. Three days' growth of beard covered his hollow cheeks. His eye sockets were as deep and dark as drain holes. His shirt was stained and ripped, and his pants were filthy. Across from him, damp as he was, Goémond seemed almost impeccable.

"A couple of hours from now," said Treuffais, "your superiors will have put an end to this farce."

"Maybe."

"Buenaventura Diaz will not be coming here now," Treuffais reiterated.

"He will come and kill you, you little shit. I know his type. Once they start killing, they can't stop."

"He's already in Italy, you moron," said Treuffais.

"In Italy? Why Italy?"

"Or in Belgium," said Treuffais.

"Shut up, faggot. I'm trying to think."

"Good idea. Listen, I'll recite you a poem. What would you like, classical or baroque?"

"Shut the fuck up!" said Goémond. "Shut up! When someone rings the doorbell, in a while or even tomorrow, I take the cuffs off, and you go and answer. You open the door. It will be your only chance to get out of this alive."

"Nobody is going to ring the doorbell," said Treuffais, and then went on:

> O Rose, thou art sick:
> The invisible worm,
> That flies in the night
> In the howling storm,
> Has found out thy bed
> Of crimson joy

"Are you going to close your trap, asshole?" asked Goémond as he rose from the armchair and smashed his heel repeatedly into the face of his prisoner.

# 40

BUENAVENTURA had walked into the building next door. He had climbed the stairs to the top. Directly above the last landing was a trapdoor that opened onto the roof. It was secured with a kind of lock that to pick would require tools. The Catalan considered forcing it, but the trap was high up and he had nothing to stand on to reach it. The young man went down a corridor past mansarded maids' rooms, gently trying each door in turn. The third handle turned. Buenaventura pushed the door ajar. In the shadows he discerned someone sleeping in a narrow bed. He waited for the timer on the stairwell light, which he had activated when coming up, to shut off. Then he crept into a room vaguely lit up by the city lights continually flashing through the dormer window.

The occupant of the narrow bed was snoring. Buenaventura went over for a closer look. It was an old man, unkempt and financially insecure, to judge by his rank odor. He was sleeping like a baby.

The Catalan left the side of the bed, cautiously opened the window, and, clambering over a whitewood commode, got out onto the ledge. There he performed further gymnastics in order to return the Erma to the lining of his coat. Around the dormer, slates rose at a gentle incline to a flat roof. Once both his hands were free, Buenaventura let go of the window and laid his thin body down flat on the moist slates. Their moistness worked to his advantage. The temperature was only just below freezing, so water was not yet ice, not yet slippery but instead somehow adhesive. Inching his way along, Buenaventura crawled all the way to the edge of the flat rooftop. He reached it but remained prone, his eyes plumbing the shadows. Chimneys, television antennae. No sign of any human life. The Catalan hesitated for a moment, then decided to get up onto the roof terrace. Patches of gravel crunched beneath the soles of his sneakers.

Still nobody. Buenaventura was nervous. He imagined a horde of cops watching his every move. Or else, was it possible that they were all in Treuffais's stairwell? Or again, could it be that he was mistaken and that there was no trap, no Treuffais, no commissioner at all?

He quickly stepped over the low divider separating the rooftop he had reached from its neighbor. Now he was standing on the roof of Treuffais's building.

Nothing. Nobody. The chimneys and antennae were stockstill in the dark and Buenaventura dismissed the notion that they were looking at him mockingly. He consulted his watch, which he had wound and set to the right time at the Ventrée weekend house. Four in the morning. The proletariat was sleeping with one eye open in its suburbs; middle managers for their part were sleeping like dumb logs in their luxury co-ops overlooking the Seine. The late-night pizzerias in Saint-Germain-des-Prés were closing up and shooing out languid, ravishing transvestites. Daughters of the well-to-do, stupefied by drink and hashish, were getting fucked in Paris's western outskirts and faking orgasms to mask their nausea. Bums were passing around venereal diseases under the bridges. La Coupole had closed, and intellectuals were parting company at the Raspail-Montparnasse intersection and promising to phone one another. At the printing houses the Linotypists were working away. Headlines concerning the killings of the morning before were being composed. Editorials had been delivered with headlines varying according to the opinion of the particular paper: WHY? or BLOOD or HOW FAR WILL IT GO? or VICIOUS CIRCLE or FOOLHARDY JOE BLOW VS. STORM TROOPERS IN PEAK FORM. Buenaventura was cautiously rounding each chimney for fear of being shot in the back.

Once he was sure there was no cat and no cop abroad on the roof, he felt perplexed. His perplexity did not encourage him to venture down Treuffais's stairs. He set to work instead on the television antennae. Taking the guylines that prevented them from swaying or breaking in high winds, he tied them end to end with fiercely tight knots. The long cable that he created in this way was terribly slippery because the guys were sheathed in plastic. Buenaventura lashed one end securely around a chimney stack, set himself up to rappel, and launched himself into the void above the street. His right hand, around which he had twisted the line, ensured that he descended slowly. He went spiderlike down the front of the building until he reached Treuffais's floor. The soles of his sneakers silently grazed the balcony before achieving a firm footing. He stood outside the windows, through which he could see the living room, dimly illuminated by the kitchen lights, and two silhouetted figures not looking his way.

# 41

"You still haven't found Goémond?"

"No, sir."

"Have you tried going to the home of the Treuffais guy? Marcel Treuffais?"

"No, sir."

"So go there. What are you waiting for?"

"Nothing, sir. As you wish, sir."

# 42

BUENAVENTURA Diaz burst through the living-room window screaming with joy and despair. He held the sawed-off carbine in his left hand and, as shards of glass still showered down around him, dropped to one knee and opened fire on Goémond, operating the Erma's lever with his right hand. The .22 LR bullets hit the commissioner in the back. He was precipitated forward. His forehead struck the frame of the communicating door. Rebounding, he flung himself down on his stomach behind the father's armchair, which bullets continued to fill with holes.

As he was wearing a bulletproof vest, the commissioner was shaken up but unwounded.

The Erma's firing pin clicked on empty and Buenaventura threw the carbine into the middle of the room and with his left hand drew his automatic.

"Death to pigs!" he cried just as Goémond fired at him around the armchair and shattered his elbow.

Buenaventura screamed and whirled, executing a full turn on his heels. Goémond put another bullet in his chest with the Colt Cobra. The Catalan's lung burst and he fell backwards, crashed into the window and collapsed onto his back. He felt under his trench coat with his right hand. His pistol was lying in the middle of the threadbare carpet.

Goémond uttered a cry of glee and dashed towards the terrorist, Cobra in hand.

"Long live death!" said Buenaventura as he withdrew the shortened Charlin from the left-side lining of his trench coat and emptied the two barrels into the policeman's face.

At such close quarters the shot fused into a single projectile that demolished and removed Goémond's head. Fragments of bone and brains and tufts of hair hurtled through the air like the grand finale of a fireworks display, then splattered onto and adhered to the ceiling, the floor and the walls. The commissioner's headless body sailed into the air with feet together before flopping down on its back in the middle of the room with a squelch. Buenaventura tossed the sawed-off aside and started to vomit blood.

"Buen," called Treuffais. "Are you hit?"

"I'm finished," gurgled the Catalan.

Treuffais struggled frantically, reached the commissioner's decapitated corpse and went through the policeman's pockets. He found the keys to the handcuffs. Buenaventura lay unmoving beneath the window, his chin on his chest, as a rosy stream flowed from his mouth and nose and stained his white sweater, his hunting jacket, and his trench coat. Being of pulmonary origin, the blood was full of bubbles and it foamed like spilt beer.

"The tapes are in my jacket pockets," said the wounded man.

"What are you saying?"

The Catalan made no reply. Treuffais unlocked his cuffs and hurried to his friend's side, stepping over Goémond's corpse. He knelt down next to Buenaventura, who looked at him for a moment without a word and then died.

"Farewell, dumbass," said Treuffais, and his eyes brimmed with tears. Sobs shook him so violently that he began to retch.

He got up and opened the apartment door. The light was on in the stairwell. Neighbors were calling out to one another from one floor to the next. There was talk of gunshots, telephoning, police emergency services. Treuffais returned to his apartment, bolted the door, and went over to the telephone. He dialed the number of a foreign press agency, asked to speak to a reporter, and was put through to one.

Through the broken windowpanes came the dismal whine of fast-approaching police vans.

"Listen, man, and take careful notes," said Treuffais, eyeing the corpses. "I am going to tell you the short but complete history of the Nada group."

# OTHER NEW YORK REVIEW CLASSICS

*For a complete list of titles, visit www.nyrb.com or write to:*
*Catalog Requests, NYRB, 435 Hudson Street, New York, NY 10014*

*\* Also available as an electronic book.*

**FÉLIX FÉNÉON** Novels in Three Lines*

**M.I. FINLEY** The World of Odysseus

**THOMAS FLANAGAN** The Year of the French*

**BENJAMIN FONDANE** Existential Monday: Philosophical Essays*

**SANFORD FRIEDMAN** Conversations with Beethoven*

**MARC FUMAROLI** When the World Spoke French

**CARLO EMILIO GADDA** That Awful Mess on the Via Merulana

**BENITO PÉREZ GÁLDOS** Tristana*

**MAVIS GALLANT** Paris Stories*

**MAVIS GALLANT** Varieties of Exile*

**GABRIEL GARCÍA MÁRQUEZ** Clandestine in Chile: The Adventures of Miguel Littín

**LEONARD GARDNER** Fat City*

**WILLIAM H. GASS** On Being Blue: A Philosophical Inquiry*

**THÉOPHILE GAUTIER** My Fantoms

**GE FEI** The Invisibility Cloak

**JEAN GENET** Prisoner of Love

**ÉLISABETH GILLE** The Mirador: Dreamed Memories of Irène Némirovsky by Her Daughter*

**NATALIA GINZBURG** Family Lexicon*

**FRANÇOISE GILOT** Life with Picasso*

**JEAN GIONO** Hill*

**JEAN GIONO** A King Alone*

**JOHN GLASSCO** Memoirs of Montparnasse*

**P.V. GLOB** The Bog People: Iron-Age Man Preserved

**NIKOLAI GOGOL** Dead Souls*

**EDMOND AND JULES DE GONCOURT** Pages from the Goncourt Journals

**ALICE GOODMAN** History Is Our Mother: Three Libretti*

**PAUL GOODMAN** Growing Up Absurd: Problems of Youth in the Organized Society*

**EDWARD GOREY (EDITOR)** The Haunted Looking Glass

**JEREMIAS GOTTHELF** The Black Spider*

**A.C. GRAHAM** Poems of the Late T'ang

**JULIEN GRACQ** Balcony in the Forest*

**HENRY GREEN** Blindness*

**HENRY GREEN** Caught*

**HENRY GREEN** Loving*

**HENRY GREEN** Party Going*

**WILLIAM LINDSAY GRESHAM** Nightmare Alley*

**HANS HERBERT GRIMM** Schlump*

**EMMETT GROGAN** Ringolevio: A Life Played for Keeps

**VASILY GROSSMAN** Everything Flows*

**VASILY GROSSMAN** Life and Fate*

**VASILY GROSSMAN** Stalingrad*

**LOUIS GUILLOUX** Blood Dark*

**OAKLEY HALL** Warlock

**PATRICK HAMILTON** The Slaves of Solitude*

**PETER HANDKE** Short Letter, Long Farewell

**THORKILD HANSEN** Arabia Felix: The Danish Expedition of 1761–1767*

**ELIZABETH HARDWICK** The Collected Essays of Elizabeth Hardwick*

**ELIZABETH HARDWICK** Sleepless Nights*

**NATHANIEL HAWTHORNE** Twenty Days with Julian & Little Bunny by Papa

**ALFRED HAYES** In Love*

**PAUL HAZARD** The Crisis of the European Mind: 1680–1715*

**WOLFGANG HERRNDORF** Sand*

**RUSSELL HOBAN** Turtle Diary*